綠野仙蹤

成寒英語有聲書 ①

成寒◎編著

這部《綠野仙蹤》是由經典名著改編的舞台劇，角色鮮明，情節生動活潑，CD共有18段。

學習方法：

請參閱成寒著

《英文，非學好不可》

及《早早開始，慢曼來》兩本書。

〔推薦序〕

在英文的天空單飛

侯文詠

　　學英文大家都有經驗，但是學好英文的經驗卻很少聽人說過。成寒從一開始英文不好，到托福考滿分，甚至還跑到美國去學英語教學，不說學歷、資格，光是這個經驗就很值得一聽。

　　歸納起來，成寒的英文學習經驗不難，問題是過去台灣的英語學習從來不強調，你要說它是革命性的學習法也沒有什麼不可。很多人聽到「革命性」眼睛睜得大大的，以為有什麼天大的祕訣，說穿了沒什麼──那就是學英文先從「聽」力開始。

　　我曾經有過一次扮演視障的經驗，從台北坐車到新莊。那次的經驗讓我發現，人對視覺的依賴真是驚人。扮演盲人的經驗讓我感受到了不同時空下的氣味，聲音差別，甚至是汽車經過橋樑，橋面接縫規律的跳動……這些都是過去坐車時不曾感受過的。這讓我體會到視覺固然提供了方便，但過分強調視覺的生物本能壓抑了其他的感覺。

　　回想學語言的經驗，其實也是一樣。從前我的祖母不認識字，她的國語全從中視最早《晶晶》、《情旅》、《春雷》這些國語連續劇裡面學來。那時候連續劇裡有個可憐的晶晶，每天一個小時用國語在電視裡面找媽媽。我的祖母很著迷那齣戲，她先是要我逐句口譯成台語，搞得我煩不勝煩，後來她自己慢慢學會「聽」懂了一些國語。晶晶總是和面對面媽媽擦身而過，彼此不認識。我的祖母也跟著驚歎、流眼淚。晶晶就這樣找啊找了一、二百天，我的祖母也漸漸不太需要口譯，一個不認識字的老太太就這樣學會了「聽」國語，看懂了接下來的《情旅》、《春雷》大部分的劇情和對白……

　　這樣的經驗再回來看目前的鄉土教學就覺得很挫折。我最近看到台北的小孩子用注音的方式學閩南語，實在是很可憐。他們說台語像是學英文背單字一樣，不但如此，音標還會弄錯……我們的老大閩南語說得還算可以，他小時候被丟在南部阿公阿媽家，每天去鄉下的學校和學生一起上課、玩耍，一個暑假就學會了說閩南語，不但如此，到現在愈說愈流利……

　　有了這樣的經驗，我教我們家小孩學英文是從聽力先開始的。我記得我們從前學英文不是這樣。好比說考單字吧，以草原 prairie【prɛrɪ】為例，我們那時候叫文意字彙，得先

背拼法，好不容易背出來了，又要考音標，結果搞不清楚 ai
到底發成【e】、【aɪ】還是【ɛ】，因此自小雖然學了一堆單
字，要用時根本開不了口。我教自己的小孩學英文反過來，
我要小孩先聽懂這個單字，自己把課文唸出來，並且錄音，
最後父母親再聽錄音來糾正他。一旦小孩會唸之後，背草原
這個單字時基本上他已經會了 pr【ɛ】r【ɪ】，他只要注意一
下是　pr-ai-r-ie，單字就迎刃而解了。方法看起來好像差不
多，開始做以後就會發現差別很大，因為這些母音與字母拼
法間有一定的規則，小孩背單字時只要對照一下規則，注意
個別字母特殊的拼法，背起單字比別人快也比別人容易。

　　從聽力入手學英文還有一個很大的優勢。那就是，不像
「視覺」，大部分時間我們的「聽覺」其實是空閒的。我相信
在每天交通的時間、等待的時間、一個人獨處的時間，甚至
是慢跑、運動的時間，「聽」一些什麼遠比「讀」些什麼容
易很多。這幾年，視聽科技的發展驚人，各式各樣的
MP3、WMA 播放器又小又輕便，很容易就買到。目前我自
己就有一台 ipod 隨身聽，有著七千多首歌曲的容量。除了把
CD 轉換成 MP3 隨身聽外，還可以上許多類似像是
Audible.com 這樣的網站，購買最新出版的英文有聲書下
載。我從來就不相信語言學習中有所謂聰明不聰明的問題。
語言學習並不是大腦皮質層的理解，說穿了是重複和反射的

一種持續練習，因此祕訣在於如何把自己置身於那種豐富的語言環境裡。這幾年，利用這些隨身的新科技，我聽了不少英文，偶爾我會翻翻書，把那幾個一直聽到的單字弄清楚。除此之外，我真的很少覺得自己花了時間，用力學過英文。或許利用聽覺空間，以及有聲書本身的趣味性，使得語言學習不再那麼困難。

我另外一個受成寒影響的觀念就是聽英文有聲書、演講、廣播劇……她甚至主張你在看《慾望城市》時把 DVD 的字幕關掉，好讓自己能夠體會都會性十足的生活美語。這種完全沒有任何輔助的英文單飛經驗，對很多人來說實在是抗拒性十足。至少在我們家的情況正是如此。

「喔，那會多麼沒有樂趣？」，「看不懂怎麼辦？」

老實說我也不知道看不懂該怎麼辦？我在電影這件事的經驗是：很難看不懂。只要聽得懂百分之三、四十的對白，大概你就能掌握整個劇情了。萬一你連百分之三、四十都沒有的話，也不會怎樣嘛──至少沒有人會笑你。你隨時還可以打開字幕再看第二次，之後甚至關掉字幕再看第三次。從看電影的角度，沒有字幕當然很討厭。可是從學英文的角度，你實在找不出更有趣的辦法來了。我的建議是，一旦你不得不這樣做時，你可以說服自己，你利用的是學英文的時間，而不是看電影的時間。真的不騙人，只要這樣開始做，

多看幾部之後，你很容易就發現看沒有字幕的英文電影其實也不是多麼困難的事情。

這個經驗使我聯想起家裡小孩剛開始學單車時，單車後方有兩個小小的外加輔助輪。等到小孩單車適應得差不多時，就必須拿掉那兩個輔助輪。一開始拿掉輔助輪時，老大欣然接受，老二則是哭哭啼啼。兩種不同的態度當然和他們對單車本身的想望以及害怕跌跤的恐懼有關。儘管態度不同，不過拿掉輔助輪之後，幾個小時的摸索，以及三、四次並不怎麼可怕的摔跤——兩個孩子需要的時間是差不多的。

幾次練習之後，兩個孩子現在都體會到了單飛的樂趣，沒有人想再使用輔助輪了。我有時候會想，學語言何嘗不也是這樣呢？其實大部分人只差一些摸索的時間以及幾次不怎麼可怕的摔跤就能單飛了，不知道為什麼，就是在拿掉輔助輪的前一剎那裹足不前？

最後回到《綠野仙蹤》（畢竟這篇文章是因它開始的）。我說它真是個有趣的英語舞台劇。不過除了有趣之外，我覺得成寒最想示範的就是在語言學習中，那種單飛的感覺。（也許還有幾次不怎麼可怕的摔跤）。

當然，更重要的是在這之前的那一剎那，拿掉輔助輪的熱情和勇氣。

＊沿著黃磚道一直走去，翡翠城就會出現在眼前。

學英語像吟詩、說故事
——關於成寒英語有聲書

《躺著學英文》第一、二、三集不斷強調聽力的重要，聽得懂，才會說，也會寫。單字及片語聽熟了，也比較容易記住。學英語，就是要活學活用，而不是背得死去活來。

這一系列《成寒英語有聲書》，教讀者從故事中學到一點文化、一些知識或理念，在不知不覺中學會了字彙、片語及文法。

「聽」是個連續性、不間斷的活動，除非你故意按下「暫停鍵」，不然「聽」就是一直聽下去。長期聽英語，可以培養英文快速理解力，不必分析，也不用思考，聽到的同時已在腦海裡轉換成資訊，毋需經過中翻英或英翻中的過程。

就像跳舞、運動都要培養韻律感，學英語不該只專注在字彙上。看著音標自己發音，「咬文嚼字」說出的英語顯得做作且彆扭。學英語應該模仿「英語人士」的「口音」（accent）和「腔調」（intonation），培養對高低輕重音不同的感覺；一如聽歌，旋律比個別字句還重要。

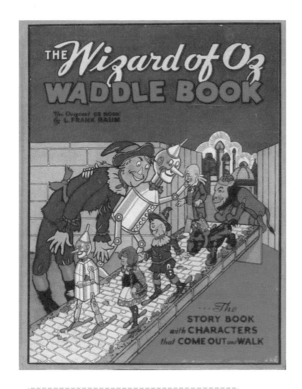

＊會走動的立體人物書《綠野仙蹤》封面，錫樵夫、桃樂絲、稻草人、托托、膽小獅及奧茲，依序排列走在黃磚道上。

＊　　＊　　＊

美麗的韓國女星金玟說：「哎呀！糗大了。」

金玟以前當記者時曾鬧過笑話。有一天她去採訪一位男星，事先她看著英文名字拼音，以為要採訪的對象是什麼「秋論花」，心裡想這是哪位仁兄，名字連聽都沒聽過。

直到見了本尊，她才恍然大悟，原來是國際巨星「周潤發」。

＊　　＊　　＊

一個朋友是空中小姐，有回飛到某個非英語系國家過夜。旅館裡只有一個頻道放映英語電影，於是當晚每一位空中小姐和空中少爺都看了同一部電影。

可是，第二天用早餐時，大家討論片子的内容及結局，發現每個人的答案都不一樣。

* * *

為何有些人學了多年英語，還是沒辦法聽得懂英語電影？

或者，當一個老美跟你說話時，你聽得懂，因為他會配合你；但當一群老美自己在聊天時，你聽不懂，因此插不上嘴。這不是你的英語程度不好（因為那些單字你大部分都認得），而是「口音」及「腔調」的適應問題。

我剛回台灣時，隔著電話，有些人的國語五句我有兩句聽不懂。因為在美國多年，我很少聽台灣人說話。而出國以前，一個內向的小女生來往的人實在不多，又從來不看電視或聽收音機。

* * *

《成寒英語有聲書》是「正常速度」的英語，

* 《綠野仙蹤》第一版在一九○○年推出，至今已超過一百年。

讓讀者一口氣聽下來,先享受聽故事的樂趣,再細讀文中的單字及片語的用法,學著開口說,然後試著寫。

如果你學的是「慢速」的學習英語,而非「正常速度」的英語,那你的英語程度永遠停滯在某個程度,進步有限。

如果為了考試,把英語肢解成一字字或一句句,學到的只是「斷簡殘篇」,把英語弄得索然無味。聽故事,好聽的有聲書,是學英語的好方法。把學英語當吟詩、說故事,就是這麼自然,這麼簡單。

《綠野仙蹤》這本書能夠順利推出,在此誠摯感謝寫專文推薦的侯文詠先生;刊登本書導讀的《國語日報》主編孫莉莉小姐、《明道文藝》社長陳憲仁先生;刊登英語 Key words 解說的《中國時報》〈浮世繪〉版主編夏瑞紅小姐、《國語日報》〈青春版〉主編林敏束小姐;好友紀元文博士的校正;以及時報出版公司總編輯林馨琴、主編張敏敏、編輯林文理三位女士。

＊「會走動的立體人物書」（waddle book）：似玩偶的人物造形,可以移動；「立體書」（pop-up book）：把書翻開即成立體造形,但無法取出移動。

＊有關英文學習的問題,歡迎上成寒網站:
www.chenhen.com

《綠野仙蹤》的奇幻世界

你看過《綠野仙蹤》（*The Wizard of Oz*）這部電影或這本書嗎？

英國女作家羅琳（J.K. Rowling）筆下的《哈利波特》（*Harry Potter*）把每一位讀者帶入神奇的魔幻境界，眩目而迷離。可是你知道嗎？早在一百多年前，風靡全世界老少讀者的《綠野仙蹤》，書裡就出現一雙神奇的魔法鞋，只要讓兩鞋跟互相輕叩三下，嘴裡唸出咒語，它就會帶你到任何想去的地方。

第一部美國童話

一九三九年，米高梅公司將《綠野仙蹤》（*The Wonderful Wizard of Oz*）原著改編成電影，英文片名拿掉"Wonderful"一字。為了強調戲劇效

＊電影《綠野仙蹤》裡的那雙紅鞋子。

果，把書中的銀鞋子（silver shoes）改成了紅鞋子──紅寶石便鞋（ruby slippers）。

《綠野仙蹤》英文原著於一九○○年推出，一百多年來一直是極受歡迎的奇幻魔法書。在此前，美國兒童閱讀的童話故事都是從歐陸來的，如德國格林童話、丹麥安徒生童話。這是第一部美國童話。

《綠野仙蹤》的主角是個小女孩，名叫桃樂絲，頭髮中分，綁成兩把可愛的小馬尾。桃樂絲是個孤女，從小就被叔叔和嬸嬸收養，定居在堪薩斯州。

堪薩斯是個民風純樸的鄉下地方，居民務農，安份守己，大部分人一輩子都沒有離開過家鄉。攤開美國地圖，你會發現，堪薩斯州的位置不偏不倚就在美國的正中央，往東和往西是一樣遠；往南和往北，也是同等距離。這塊地

＊KS：堪薩斯的簡寫，位於美國本土的正中央。

方由於地勢廣闊又平坦，龍捲風常成群出現，一個接一個，強風所到之處氣壓猛烈下降，尤其是高層和低層的水平風向、風速顯著差異，在雷暴強烈上升的垂直氣流影響下，將水平旋轉的氣柱扭轉成垂直旋轉的龍捲風。

有一天，突起的龍捲風，將小女孩桃樂絲及小狗托托連人帶房子一起捲入暴風圈中，一陣天旋地轉，剎那間昏天暗地，而且越捲越高，越捲越遠……窗外一片漆黑，什麼也看不見。

待房子落地後，桃樂絲發現自己來到神祕仙境「奧茲國」（The Land of Oz），而在房子底下卻壓死了一個壞巫婆……。桃樂絲帶著小狗托托沿著黃磚路行去，一路上遇到稻草人、錫樵夫及膽小獅，他們一道前往翡翠城向魔法師奧茲請願，求他賜給他們一個聰明的頭腦、一顆心、一份勇氣，途中他們又碰上好巫婆和壞巫婆，迭經多重歷險，桃樂絲終於回到堪薩斯的家。

＊翡翠城裡住著一位神奇的奧茲魔法師。

　　據說，在《綠野仙蹤》拍片過程中，幕後工作人員為女主角茱蒂‧迦倫（Judy Garland）準備了至少七雙一模一樣的紅鞋子，有四雙依然留存至今。其中一雙紅鞋子，目前永久陳列於華府的史密森博物館（Smithsonian Institution）美國史陳列館。

Oz的由來

　　《綠野仙蹤》按原文直譯「奧茲魔法師」。至於「OZ」這兩個字的靈感，究竟從何而來？

　　許多讀者都相信，那是在一八九八年五月七日晚，作者法蘭克‧鮑姆（L. Frank Baum）四十二歲生日的前八天，那時他正在說故事，孩子們個個聽得入了迷。

　　其中一個孩子問：「鮑姆先生，請問那個奇幻的地方叫什麼名字？」

　　鮑姆頓了頓，環顧四周，然後眼光停格在屋角檔案櫃的抽屜，最上層標示著：「A－N」，最底層則標示著：「O－Z」。啊哈，這就是「奧茲」的由來！

應讀者要求，一共寫了十四本

　　鮑姆一八五六年生於紐約州，從小身體虛弱，個性害羞

＊《綠野仙蹤》作者法蘭克・鮑姆，時年二十一。
他的岳母曾經形容他：「一無是處的夢想家！」

內向，喜歡幻想，怪點子奇多。

鮑姆一八九九年撰寫《綠野仙蹤》之際，大概沒有料到這本書會如此受歡迎，歷久不衰。由於故事被改編成舞台劇、音樂劇、默片、有聲電影、冰上舞劇、卡通動畫以及一連串電視劇集，家喻戶曉，連從來沒看過書的人都知道故事的內容。但《綠野仙蹤》其實只是第一本書而已，鮑姆一共寫了十四本有關OZ系列。他死後，還有更多的作者接棒，整個OZ全集甚至多達四十冊！

迪士尼公司在一九八五年曾將第二及第三集拍成特效極佳的《天魔歷險》（*Return to Oz*）。連歌手艾爾頓・強（Elton John）也出過一套唱片專集《再見，黃磚道》（*Goodbye Yellow Brick Road*）。

　　書的內容和電影略有不同，在電影裡，桃樂絲前往奧茲國的歷險記發生在夢裡，只是想像，並非真有其事。然而在書中卻是真實的，讓孩童盡情發揮其想像力，彷彿真有奧茲這地方，就在彩虹之上，充滿著希望，讓孩子在閱讀中逃離平凡的、不滿意的人生。

綠野仙蹤，賭城重現

　　二○○二年春節我到賭城拉斯維加斯（Las Vegas），一時興起走入米高梅大飯店（MGM Grand Hotel）參觀。這座飯店有三座三十層高樓，內有五千多個客房，由米高梅電影公司出資建造，一九九三年十二月十八日開幕。翡翠綠的外觀，入口大廳以一隻趴著的獅子作屋頂，一看分明是《綠野仙蹤》裡的角色──膽小獅。

　　飯店內，《綠野仙蹤》的主題隨處可見：入口處，迎面有一座如夢似幻的翡翠城（可惜，後來重新整修時已拆除），擺著幾個以劇中主角造形製成會動的玩偶，還鋪了一條黃磚道，設置紅鞋子造形的吃角子老虎機、飛天猴酒吧以及壁上的連環畫，連走廊的地毯、房間裡的床單也是書中罌粟花田的圖案，還有打扮成桃樂絲、稻草人、錫樵夫、膽小獅等的服務員與兒童拍照留念。

先有夢想，然後成真

　　說到鮑姆，他小時候害羞、孤獨。因為心臟不好，不能出外運動，大半時間都待在屋裡看書，看童話故事，與幻想中的朋友作玩伴。然而日後他表示：「小時候我並不喜歡童話故事，因為充滿了恐怖。」這些童話故事害他作惡夢，所以他要寫的是不一樣的童話故事。

　　鮑姆一生曾經辦過報紙和雜誌，也開過百貨店和管理過企業，但最成功的事業就是寫書。說故事

＊童年時期的法蘭克‧鮑姆，害羞、孤獨，與幻想中的朋友作玩伴。

的能力，鮑姆似乎與生俱來──他就是有抓住孩童想像力的本事。鮑姆在他另一本奧茲系列故事的前言寫道：「因為有想像力，人類才會發明蒸汽機、電話和汽車，先有夢想，然後成真。因此，我認為作夢，白日夢或不管什麼夢……夢想

打開你的眼睛……夢想讓世界更美好，文明更進步。」

鮑姆寫《綠野仙蹤》，就是要讓兒童一掃憂傷和鬼魅的陰影，故事帶來的是希望而不是惡夢。因此，《綠野仙蹤》全書充滿風趣幽默、氣氛明朗愉悅，沒有暴力和恐怖情節，一波波的冒險高潮迭起，但卻充滿正面的、樂觀的意識。

鮑姆其實也想寫些別的主題，如《鵝爸爸》（Father Goose）出版於一八九九年，接著是《鵝媽媽》（Mother Goose），皆暢銷一時。他也以別的筆名寫了好幾本書。然而，任何一本書的銷售量都及不上《綠野仙蹤》。何況孩子們不斷寫信給他，說他們如何為《綠野仙蹤》著迷，求他再寫更多更多的故事。不僅是小孩，連大人也喜歡呢。

他說：「我的書是為那些擁有年輕心靈的讀者而寫的，不管他們的年紀有多大。」

而鮑姆這個人，不

＊鮑姆另一部受歡迎的作品《鵝爸爸》。

做則已，一旦他決定要做一件事，就很投入，這是他的人生哲學。晚年遷至加州好萊塢，有人把他的家叫做「奧茲居」（Ozcot）。鮑姆把心思投入園藝上也得到同樣的成果，他竟以種大理花和雛菊知名，在南加州獲得多項園藝獎。

＊鮑姆一生最後的家，位於加州好萊塢，有人叫它「奧茲居」。

晚年，雖然病痛纏身，他依然躺在床上墊枕頭寫作，第十四部也是最後一部奧茲系列故事在一九二〇年，他死後次年才問世。

每個人都是獨一無二的

　　《綠野仙蹤》表面上只是一個精采有趣的童話故事，但背後卻有更深的涵意。

　　在這世上，許多人對自己沒有信心，甚至有強烈的自卑感，覺得自己比別人差，對自我存著懷疑，以為自己一無所長，平凡得不值一提。但事實上，每個人都是「獨一無二的」（unique），有些長處，只是一時沒有發揮出來罷了。

　　一如本書改編電影的女主角茱蒂‧迦倫，長得嬌俏美麗，人人眼中的標準美女，在電影中飾演女主角桃樂絲。她

＊《綠野仙蹤》電影中的女主角茱蒂‧迦倫及小黑狗托托曾登上美國郵票。

的女兒是著名女星兼歌手麗莎‧明妮莉（Liza Minnelli），是她和第二任丈夫名導演文生‧明尼利（Vincente Minnelli）所生。當茱蒂‧迦倫吟唱起《綠野仙蹤》主題曲：〈在彩虹之上的地方〉（Somewhere Over the Rainbow），幾乎讓每個人聽得入迷。可是她的一生因缺乏自信，不斷地掙扎，對自己存疑，活得一點也不快樂。

桃樂絲的三個同伴——稻草人、錫樵夫和膽小獅，每個都覺得自己少了什麼，如稻草人一心想抽掉稻草，換新的腦袋；錫樵夫需要一顆跳動的心；膽小獅則希望有勇氣，有朝一日成為名副其實的萬獸之王。桃樂絲則一心想回家。

一個好心的女巫告訴她，只要找到偉大的「奧茲魔法師」，再難的問題都能解決。然而，從來沒有人真正親眼見過魔法師本人。

沒有一個地方比得上自己的家

當桃樂絲一行人親眼見到魔法師本尊，發現他不過是個矮小的、禿頭的傢伙，難怪他從來不肯露臉，不讓別人親眼見到他的廬山真面目。別人尊崇他，乃因將他視為盲目的信仰。當桃樂絲等人終於發現魔法師是個「騙子」或「冒牌貨」，這段情節帶給讀者一些啟示，也是對一些裝模作樣、本身並非真有多麼了不起的人極大的諷刺。

然而，魔法師也一語點醒了這一行人。他說稻草人能想方設法，表示他的確有腦袋；錫樵夫心地善良，證明他本來就有心；而膽小獅勇敢幫助眾人，意謂著他具有勇氣，

而「家」，在故事中也有象徵性的意義。儘管翡翠城綠意盎然、百花綻放，桃樂絲一心還是想回家，回到單調枯燥的中西部平原上的家。為了顯示堪薩斯的單調，電影前面一段還故意以黑白畫面呈現。歷經一番冒險，到處跌跌撞撞，桃樂絲最後才發現，原來回家的路子就在她自己。她腳上穿的那雙具有魔法力的紅鞋子，只要讓兩鞋跟互相輕叩三下，嘴裡不斷唸著，她就立刻回到家：

There's no place like home！

沒有任何地方，比得上自己的家好！

金窩、銀窩比不上自己的狗窩！

魔法就是你自己的想像力

你相信「魔法」（magic）嗎？這個世界上，到底有沒有魔法？其實，魔法自在人心。真正的魔法，存在於個人的心裡；你相信有，那就是有。因為，魔法就是你的「想像力」（imagination）。

一九一九年五月五日，鮑姆在加州離開人世。他生前曾經說過：「只要你相信有奧茲的存在，那麼它就真的存在，也許存在於世上某個角落；奧茲代表著夢想，只要有夢，它就會實現。」

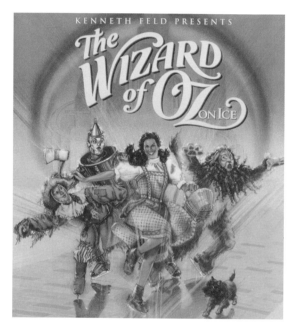

鮑姆筆下的銀鞋子以及電影中的紅鞋子，雖然是虛構的、不存在的，但它代表著夢想。也許，每個小女孩小男孩的心目中都有一雙魔法鞋，只要輕叩幾下鞋跟，它會帶妳到任何想去的地方，追尋那奇幻的、不可及的夢。

* 《綠野仙蹤》冰上舞劇海報。

* 關於《綠野仙蹤》英文原著及電影劇本，可以在「成寒」網站上免費下載：http://www.chenhen.com

* 「女巫」（witch）和「魔法師」（wizard）其實是一樣的，只是性別不同，魔法師也就是男巫師。女巫使用的巫術稱 "witchcraft"，魔法師使用的巫術稱 "wizardry"。

旁白　Narrator

亨利叔叔　Uncle Henry

桃樂絲　Dorothy

艾姆嬸嬸　Aunt Em

芒虛金　Munchkin

北方好女巫　Good Witch of the North

東方壞女巫　Wicked Witch of the East

托托　Toto

稻草人　Scarecrow

錫樵夫　Tin Woodman

膽小獅　Cowardly Lion

奧茲　Oz

西方壞女巫
Wicked Witch of the West

飛天猴　Winged Monkey

溫基人　Winkie

葛琳達
Glinda：Good Witch of the South

綠野
仙蹤

THE WIZARD OF OZ

Cyclone

CD＊1

Narrator：This is the story about the adventures of a little girl named Dorothy. She lived in the midst of the great, great Kansas prairie with her Aunt Em and Uncle Henry, who was a farmer. Their house was one room with a small hole in the ground beneath the floor, which was a cyclone cellar, where the family could be safe in case one of those great whirlwinds arose.

orothy

＊桃樂絲和她的小狗狗托
托成天玩耍，笑呵呵。

Narrator：Aunt Em and Uncle Henry never laughed, but Dorothy did, and her little black dog Toto. Toto played all day and Dorothy played with him. Today,

龍捲風

CD * 1

旁白：這是一個叫桃樂絲的小女孩的歷
險記。她與艾姆嬸嬸和亨利叔叔
住在堪薩斯大草原的中部。亨利
叔叔是農夫。他們的房子只有一
個房間，地板下有個小洞，作為
龍捲風地窖，一旦颳起巨大旋
風，一家人可以躲進去避難。

> *一陣龍捲風把房子颳上天空。

旁白：艾姆嬸嬸和亨利叔叔從來不笑，可是桃樂絲
卻笑口常開，她的小黑狗托托也是笑呵呵。
托托成天玩耍，桃樂絲也跟著牠一塊兒玩。

adventure ： n.
冒險、歷險記

name ： v.
命名

midst ： n.
中央、當中

in the midst of ：
在……中央
例： in the midst of a
crowd：在人群當中

Kansas ： n.
堪薩斯州

prairie ： n.
草原

farmer ： n.
農夫

beneath ： prep.
在……之下

cellar ： n.
地窖

in case ：
以防萬一

whirlwind ： n.
旋風

however, they weren't playing. Uncle Henry looked anxiously at the sky, which was greyer than usual. There was a low wail of wind.

Uncle Henry ： "Cyclone's coming in. I'll go look after the cattle. You and Dorothy get in the cellar there."

Narrator ： But Toto wiggled out of Dorothy's arms and ran to hide under the big bed. Dorothy ran after him.

Dorothy ： "Toto, come here."

可是，今天他們不玩耍了。亨利叔叔憂心地看著比平常灰暗的天空，一陣風低聲哀號地吹過。

亨利叔叔：「龍捲風來了，我去照顧牲畜。妳和桃樂絲快躲進地窖裡。」

旁白：然而，托托從桃樂絲的臂彎裡掙脫，躲到大床鋪底下。桃樂絲跑過去追牠。

桃樂絲：「托托，過來。」

＊桃樂絲抓住托托的耳
　朵，免得牠掉下去。

look at：
看、注視

anxiously：adv.
憂心地、渴望地

wail：n.
哀號聲、長呼聲

cyclone：n.
龍捲風。電影裡使用
"twister"字眼

look after：
照顧

cattle：n.
牲畜、牛群

wiggle：v.
扭動、擺脫

run after：
追趕

shriek：n.
哀嚎、尖叫

Narrator ： Oh, Dorothy was too late. There was a great shriek from the wind and the house shook so hard that Dorothy fell down on the floor.

旁白：哦，桃樂絲晚了一步。一陣風吹過發出尖銳的呼嘯聲，房子搖晃得太厲害，害桃樂絲跌倒在地板上。

Aunt Em ： "Dorothy! Dorothy!"

Narrator ： And then, a strange thing happened. The house rose slowly in the air.

Dorothy ： "Toto, it's like we're going up in a balloon."

Narrator ： Slowly Dorothy got over her fright and after a while she crawled over to her bed.

Dorothy ： "Oh, Toto, I'm so sleepy."

艾姆嬸嬸：「桃樂絲！桃樂絲！」

旁白：就在此時，奇怪的事發生了。房子竟悠悠緩緩地升上天空。

桃樂絲：「托托，我們好像坐氣球升空了。」

旁白：漸漸地，桃樂絲克服了她的驚駭，過了一會兒，她爬到床上。

桃樂絲：「哦，托托，我好睏。」

【sound of the wind】

Narrator ： And soon Dorothy and her little dog
were fast asleep.

【風聲】

旁白：桃樂絲和小狗狗很快進入夢鄉。

balloon ： n.
氣球

get over ：
克服

fright ： n.
驚駭

after a while ：
過了一會兒

crawl ： v.
爬行

sleepy ： adj.
想睡的、愛睏的

fast asleep ：
沈睡

fast ： adv.
深沈地

＊桃樂絲和托托很快進入
夢鄉。

The Munchkins

CD * 2

Screaming："Ahhhhh!"

Dorothy ："Toto, what was that? It was a scream! Where are we?"

【sound of yipping】

Dorothy ："We've landed somewhere. Let's look out the window. Oh, look, it's so beautiful, green trees and apples and pears and hills and butterflies and birds. Toto, look!"

Dorothy ："There is a little old woman. She is coming up here. Let's go out and say hello to her Toto, then we can find out where we are."

Dorothy ："Come on Toto."

芒虛金

CD * 2

哀嚎聲：「啊呀呀哦耶！」

桃樂絲：「托托，那是什麼？一聲尖叫！我們到底在哪裡？」

【狗汪汪叫】

桃樂絲：「我們降落在某個地方。看窗外，哦，你瞧，多美啊！綠樹、蘋果、梨子以及山丘、蝴蝶和鳥。托托，你看！」

桃樂絲：「有個小老太婆向這邊走過來，我們出去跟她打個招呼，托托。 然後，我們就可以知道身在何處。」

桃樂絲：「來吧，托托。」

scream ： n.
尖叫

land ： v.
著陸、降落

somewhere ： adv.
在某處

Dorothy ："Helloooo!"

The Good Witch of the North ："You are welcome, most noble Sorceress, to the land of the Munchkins. We are so grateful to you for having killed the Wicked Witch of the East."

＊桃樂絲遇見北方
女巫和芒虛金。

Dorothy ："Killed? I haven't killed anybody."

The Good Witch of the North ："Hahahaha! Oh, your house

桃樂絲：「哈囉！」

北方好女巫：「最高貴的女魔法師，歡迎妳來到芒
　　　　　　虛金的國度，我們非常感謝妳，因為妳殺死
　　　　　　了東方壞女巫。」

noble ： adj.
崇高的、高貴的

sorceress ： n.
女魔法師

Munchkin ： n.
芒虛金，《綠野仙蹤》
書中永遠長不高的人

grateful ： adj.
感激的

wicked ： adj.
邪惡的

witch ： n.
女巫

＊桃樂絲的房子壓在東
　方壞女巫身上。女巫
　消失了，只剩下一雙
　銀鞋子。

桃樂絲：「殺死？我不曾殺死過任何人啊。」

北方好女巫：「哈哈哈哈！哦，妳的房子壓在她身

fell on her. Hahahaha!"

Dorothy ： "That's what we heard, Toto."

The Good Witch of the North ： "See her two silver shoes? There. She's gone."

Dorothy ： "But who was she?"

The Good Witch of the North ： "She was the Wicked Witch of the East. I'm a witch too."

Dorothy ： "You are?"

The Good Witch of the North ： "Oh, yes, indeed. But I am the Good Witch of the North, and the people love me. Now there is only one Wicked Witch left, the Wicked Witch of the West."

Dorothy ： "But I thought there were no more witches."

The Good Witch of the North ： "Oh yes, oh yes, we still have witches here, and wizards."

上。哈哈哈哈！」

桃樂絲：「那就是我們聽到的聲音，托托。」

北方好女巫：「看到她那兩只銀鞋子了嗎？在那兒，她消失了。」

桃樂絲：「可是，她是誰？」

北方好女巫：「她就是東方壞女巫，我也是個女巫。」

桃樂絲：「妳是嗎？」

北方好女巫：「哦，是的，我真的是女巫。可是，我是北方好女巫，人們都喜歡我。而今，只剩一個壞女巫還活著，那就是西方壞女巫。」

桃樂絲：「可是我以為，世界上已經沒有女巫了。」

北方好女巫：「哦，有的，哦，有的，我們這裡有女巫，還有魔法師。」

fall on：
落在……上

indeed：interj.
真的、的確

no more：
不再

wizard：n.
魔法師、巫師

Dorothy："Who are the wizards?"

桃樂絲：「魔法師是什麼人？」

＊桃樂絲拿到東方壞
女巫的銀鞋子。

The Good Witch of the North ："Oz himself is the Great Wizard. He is more powerful than all the rest of us together. He lives in the City of Emeralds."

Dorothy ："Well, Mrs. Good Witch of the North, I am anxious to get back to my Aunt and Uncle. I know they're worried about me. Can you help me find my way?"

emerald ： n.
翡翠

anxious ： adj.
渴望的、急切的、
擔心的

北方好女巫：「奧茲自己就是個大魔法師，他的本事比我們所有人加起來還要強大。他住在翡翠城。」

桃樂絲：「啊，北方好女巫夫人，我急著想回到嬸嬸和叔叔的家去。我知道他們一定會擔心著我，妳能幫我找到回去的路嗎？」

＊芒虛金的個子永遠長不高，老
了以後，一個個看起來像小老
頭和小老太婆。

The Good Witch of the North："I am afraid not,
　　　　my dear. You see, a great desert surrounds
　　　　the whole Land of Oz. So I'm afraid
　　　　you're going to have to live here with us."

Dorothy："Oh, then I'll never get home again. Oh,
　　　　Toto, we'll never get home again."

【Dorothy sobs】

北方好女巫：「我恐怕沒辦法，親愛的。妳瞧，一
　　　　片遼闊的沙漠圍繞著整個奧茲國，我想妳不
　　　　得不和我們住在一起了。」

桃樂絲：「哦，那麼我永遠回不了家。哦，托托，
　　　　我們永遠不能回家了。」

【桃樂絲哭了】

desert：n.
沙漠

surround：v.
圍繞、環繞

Yellow Brick Road

CD＊3

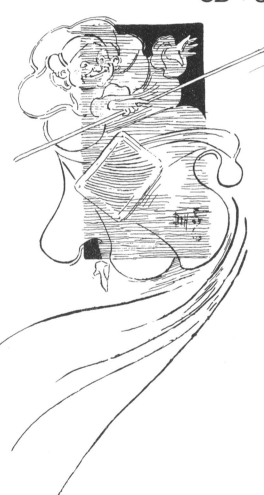

Narrator：As Dorothy sobbed, the little old woman took off her pointed cap and bounced the point on the end of her nose. At once the cap changed to a blackboard on which was written in big, white chalk:

＊北方好女巫的大黑板上面寫著白粉字：「讓桃樂絲到翡翠城去！」

黃磚道

CD ＊ 3

旁白：桃樂絲哭了，小老太婆於是取下她的尖帽
子，將尖端頂在她的鼻尖上點了一下。帽子
立刻變成一塊黑板，上面寫著巨大的白粉
字：

sob：v.
抽噎、啜泣

pointed：adj.
尖的

bounce：v.
彈起、使彈跳

at once：
立刻、馬上

blackboard：n.
黑板

chalk：n.
粉筆

＊奧茲的國度，一片青翠景象。

Dorothy：**"LET DOROTHY GO TO THE CITY OF EMERALDS!"**

Dorothy ："What does that mean?"

The Good Witch of the North ："Follow the yellow brick road. It is a long journey and sometimes very dangerous. But if you get to the City of Emeralds, the Great Oz may be able to help you."

Dorothy ："Won't you please go with me? I'm afraid."

The Good Witch of the North ："Oh, no, I cannot do that. But I will mark your brow with my kiss. No one would ever dare to injure a person who has been kissed by the Witch of the North. Here."

【sound of a kiss】

Dorothy ："Thank you."

Dorothy ："Are there any other good witches besides you?"

桃樂絲：「讓桃樂絲到翡翠城去！」

桃樂絲：「那是什麼意思？」

北方好女巫：「沿著黃磚道行去，那是一段漫長的旅程，有時很危險。但如果妳抵達翡翠城，偉大的奧茲也許能夠幫助妳。」

桃樂絲：「妳不能和我一塊兒去嗎？我會害怕。」

北方好女巫：「哦，不行，我不能那樣做。但是我可以吻妳，在妳的額頭上作記號，沒有一個人敢傷害被北方女巫吻過的人。來吧。」

【親吻聲】

桃樂絲：「謝謝妳。」

桃樂絲：「除了妳，還有別的好女巫嗎？」

journey：n.
旅程、旅行

be able to：
能夠

mark：v.
作記號

brow：n.
額頭

injure：v.
傷害

besides：prep.
除⋯⋯之外

The Good Witch of the North ："Oh, yes, there is Glinda, the Good Witch of the South. She is the most powerful of us all, except Oz. But she lives a long way off. Well, now, I must leave you. I advise you to put on those silver slippers. I am told they possess a powerful charm, perhaps they can do you good. Good-bye, my dear."

北方好女巫：「哦，有的，還有葛琳達──南方好女巫。除了奧茲以外，她是我們所有人當中力量最強大的。可是她住在遙遠的地方。啊，現在我必須離去。我勸妳穿上那雙銀鞋子，據說它們擁有強大的法術，也許對妳有好處。再會了，我親愛的。」

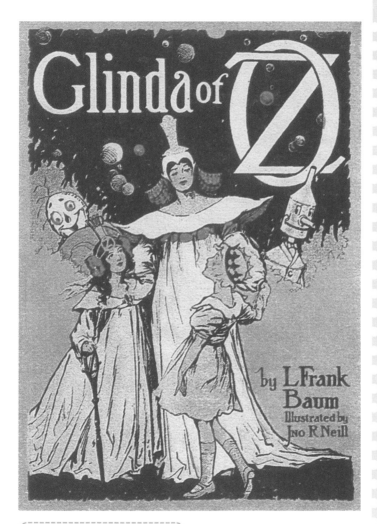

＊南方好女巫──葛琳達。

except ： prep.
除⋯⋯之外

advise ： v.
勸告、忠告

slipper ： n.
便鞋、拖鞋

possess ： v.
擁有

charm ： n.
魔力、魔法

The Scarecrow

CD * 4

Narrator ： Dorothy put on the silver slippers which fit perfectly. Then she and Toto set out on a long journey to the City of Emeralds and the Great Wizard of Oz along the yellow brick road. After she'd walked several miles, she saw a Scarecrow high on a pole in a cornfield. His blue suit was stuffed with straw. Dorothy looked into his painted face and then in surprise, she said to Toto,

Dorothy ： "Toto, that Scarecrow winked at me! And look, he is nodding. I am going over and say hello to him."

Scarecrow ： "Good day!"

Dorothy ： "Did you speak?"

Scarecrow ： "Certainly, how do you do?"

稻草人

CD * 4

旁白：桃樂絲穿上銀鞋子，剛好很合腳。然後她和托托沿著黃磚道展開漫長的旅程，前往翡翠城朝見偉大的奧茲魔法師。走了幾英里路後，她看到玉米田中有個稻草人高高掛在竹竿上。他身上穿的藍衣服裡面塞滿了稻草。桃樂絲覷一下他那張彩繪的臉，驚訝地對托托說：

桃樂絲：「托托，那個稻草人向我眨眼睛呢！瞧，他正在點頭，我要過去和他打招呼。」

稻草人：「日安！」

桃樂絲：「是你在說話嗎？」

稻草人：「當然，妳好嗎？」

put on：
穿上

fit：v.
合適

perfectly：adv.
完全地

set out：
啓程

pole：n.
竿、柱、桿

cornfield：n.
玉米田

stuff with：
塞滿

straw：n.
稻草

wink：v.
眨眼示意

nod：v.
點頭

＊玉米田中有個稻草人
高高掛在竹竿上。

Dorothy ："Huh, pretty well, thank you. How do you do?"

Scarecrow ："I'm not feeling well. This pole is stuck up my back. If you will please take me off the pole I shall be greatly obliged to you."

Dorothy ："All right."

stuck ： v.
stick 的過去式與過去
分詞，此處是過去分
詞當被動式的用法；
刺穿、穿孔

oblige ： v.
感激、感謝

＊背上沒了竹竿，稻草人覺得煥然一新。

桃樂絲：「嗯，我很好，謝謝你。你好嗎？」

稻草人：「我覺得不舒服，因為竹竿插在我的背
上。如果妳能幫我從竹竿上拆下來，我將感
激不盡。」

桃樂絲：「好吧。」

Scarecrow ： "Oh, thank you very much. Without that pole up my back, I feel like a new man. Who are you? And where are you going?"

Dorothy ： "My name is Dorothy, and I am going to the Emerald City to ask the Great Oz to send me back to Kansas."

Scarecrow ： "Where is the Emerald City?"

Dorothy ： "Don't you know?"

Scarecrow ： "No, indeed. I don't know anything. You see, I am stuffed with straw, so I have no brains at all."

Dorothy ： "Oh, I'm awfully sorry for you."

Scarecrow ： "Do you think, if I go to the Emerald City with you, that the Great Oz would give me some brains?"

Dorothy ： "I don't know, but I'd be happy to have you come with me."

稻草人：「哦，多謝妳。背上沒了竹竿，我覺得煥然一新。妳是誰？妳要去哪裡？」

桃樂絲：「我的名字叫桃樂絲，正要前往翡翠城，請求偉大的奧茲送我回堪薩斯。」

稻草人：「翡翠城在哪？」

桃樂絲：「你不知道嗎？」

稻草人：「不知道，真的，我什麼都不知道。妳瞧，我的腦袋裡塞滿了稻草，所以我一點頭腦也沒有。」

桃樂絲：「哦，我很抱歉。」

稻草人：「妳覺得，如果我和妳一塊兒到翡翠城去，那奧茲會給我一些頭腦嗎？」

桃樂絲：「我不知道，不過我很樂意你一塊兒去。」

at all ：
全然

awfully ： adv.
非常地

Scarecrow ："I don't mind being stuffed with straw, because I can't get hurt. But I don't want people to call me a fool, and with no brains, how am I ever to know anything?"

Dorothy ："I understand how you feel. Well, come along and we'll see what Oz can do for you."

Scarecrow ："Thank you."

稻草人：「我不在意腦袋裡塞滿稻草，因為我不會受傷，可是我不想讓大家叫我蠢貨。沒有頭腦，我能懂什麼？」

桃樂絲：「我明白你的感受。好吧，如果你和我們一塊兒去，我們將請求奧茲盡力幫助你。」

稻草人：「謝謝妳。」

hurt：v.
傷害、受傷

fool：n.
笨蛋、蠢貨

＊稻草人說他的腦袋
裡塞滿了稻草，所
以沒有頭腦。

Toto ："woof, woof, woof."

Dorothy ："Toto, stop that. Mr. Scarecrow, don't mind him. He never bites."

Scarecrow ："Oh, I'm not afraid. There is only one thing in the world I'm afraid of."

Dorothy ："What is that?"

Scarecrow ："A lighted match."

托托：「汪汪、汪汪、汪汪。」

桃樂絲：「托托，別那樣。稻草人先生，別理他。他從來不咬人。」

稻草人：「唔，我不怕。在這個世界上，只有一件東西令我害怕。」

桃樂絲：「那是什麼？」

稻草人：「一根點著的火柴。」

L. FRANK BAUM
"OZCOT"
AT HOLLYWOOD IN CALIFORNIA

Dec 4, 1916

My dear Carleton H. Demis

I thank you for your nice letter and the suggestions you offer. Perhaps I can use some of them, but I get so many letters asking me to do certain things that I can't possibly please all by using their valuable suggestions. However, it proves you're my friend.

Very truly yours

L. Frank Baum

＊鮑姆寫給讀者的親筆函。

bite：v.
咬

lighted：adj.
點著的

match：n.
火柴

The Tin Woodman

CD * 5

Narrator：So the three of them, Dorothy, Toto and the Scarecrow trudged down the yellow brick road together. After a while, they came to a great forest. They picked their way along until, in a clearing, they saw a little cottage. But there seemed to be no one around.

【sound of groaning】

Dorothy："What was that?"

【sound of groaning】

Dorothy："There it is again. What on earth is that? It sounds like somebody's in terrible trouble."

Scarecrow："It does indeed."

錫樵夫

CD＊5

旁白：他們一行三人，桃樂絲、托托和稻草人沿著黃磚道跋涉。過了一陣子，他們來到一座大森林。他們小心前進，來到森林中的一塊空地，看到一座小屋，可是四下似乎無人。

【呻吟聲】

桃樂絲：「那是什麼？」

【呻吟聲】

桃樂絲：「又來了，那到底是什麼？聽起來好像有人陷入很大的麻煩。」

稻草人：「顯然是的。」

trudge ： v.
以沈重的步伐前進

pick *one's* way ：
小心前進

clearing ： n.
森林中的空地

cottage ： n.
小屋

＊森林中傳來錫樵夫呻
吟的聲音。

Dorothy ："Come on, let's see if we can help. Come on, Toto."

Scarecrow ："I see something shiny over there."

Dorothy ："Yes, I see it too. It looks like a man made of tin."

＊稻草人在錫樵夫的各個關節上噴油。

shiny ： adj.
發光的

look like ：
看來像是……

made of ：
用……做成的

桃樂絲：「來吧，我們過去看看能幫上什麼忙。來
　　　　吧，托托。」

稻草人：「我看見那兒有東西閃閃發亮。」

桃樂絲：「是啊，我也看見了，看來像是一個錫造
　　　　的人。」

Dorothy ： "Excuse me, sir. Did you groan?"

The Tin Woodman ： "Yes, I did. I've been groaning for more than a year but nobody's ever heard me, because my jaws are rusted shut."

Dorothy ： "How can I help you?"

The Tin Woodman ： "Get an oil can and oil my joints. There's an oil can by my cottage."

Narrator ： Dorothy ran back to the cottage, got the oil can, and squirted oil on the Tin Woodman's joints.

〔sound of squirting〕

The Tin Woodman ： "Oh, thank you. Oh, thank you, again and again. I might have stood there for always if you had not come along."

Narrator ： Dorothy explained that they were on their way to see the Great Wizard of Oz. The Tin Woodman appeared to think deeply for a moment, and then he said,

桃樂絲：「抱歉，先生，是你在呻吟嗎？」

錫樵夫：「是的，是我。我呻吟一年多了，可是沒有人聽得到我，因為我的下顎生銹，張不開嘴巴。」

桃樂絲：「我要怎麼幫你？」

錫樵夫：「去拿一個油罐來，把油加在我的各個關節上。我的小屋旁邊有一個油罐。」

旁白：桃樂絲跑回小屋那兒，找到油罐，把油噴在錫樵夫的關節上。

【噴油的聲音】

錫樵夫：「哦，謝謝妳。哦，謝謝妳。再一次謝謝。如果你們不來的話，也許我就得永遠站在這裡了。」

旁白：桃樂絲解釋說他們正在前往晉見偉大的奧茲魔法師的路途中。錫樵夫顯然深思了一會，然後他說：

groan：v.
呻吟

jaw：n.
顎

rust：v.
使生銹

shut：adj.
閉上（此處是過去分詞當形容詞用）

can：n.
罐頭

joint：n.
關節、接合處

squirt：v.
噴出、射出

on *one's* way to：
在前往……的途中

appear：v.
看起來、顯得

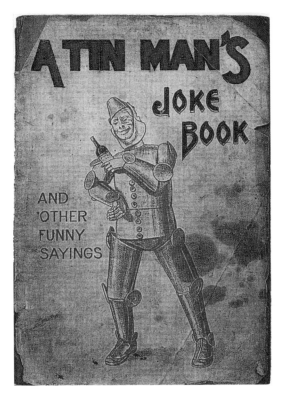

*一本《錫樵夫笑話集》。

The Tin Woodman ："Do you, do you suppose Oz could give me a heart?"

Dorothy ："Why, I guess so. Don't you have a heart?"

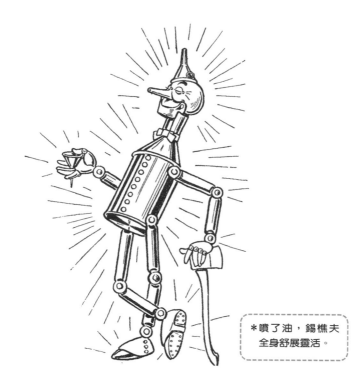

suppose ： v.
假定、推測、想像

＊噴了油，錫樵夫
全身舒展靈活。

錫樵夫：「妳，妳想奧茲可以給我一顆心嗎？」

桃樂絲：「呀，我猜想會吧。你沒有心嗎？」

The Tin Woodman ："No. You see, the tinsmith forgot to put a heart in my breast, and I truly miss it. So, if you'll allow me to join your party, I'll also go to the Emerald City, and I'll ask Oz for a heart."

Scarecrow ："Come on along."

錫樵夫：「沒有，妳看，錫匠忘了在我胸部放上一顆心，我真的很想要那顆心。因此，如果你們允許我加入一夥的話，我也要到翡翠城去，請求奧茲給我一顆心。」

稻草人：「那就走吧。」

tinsmith：n.
錫匠

breast：n.
胸部

party：n.
一群、一夥

＊錫樵夫想要一顆跳動的心。

The Cowardly Lion

CD ＊ 6

Narrator ： The yellow brick road led through a dark and scary forest. And just where it was darkest, suddenly a great beast leaped out of the trees in front of them.

【sound of roaring】

Dorothy ： "Oh, look, it's a lion, and he is as big as a horse. Oh, he's knocked over the Scarecrow."

The Tin Woodman ： "Don't worry, I'll get, uh, uh, uh, ooh, ooh..."

【sound of roaring and barking】

Dorothy ： "Don't you dare bite Toto! You ought to be ashamed of yourself, a big beast like you biting a poor little dog!"

膽小獅

CD ＊ 6

旁白：黃磚道穿過幽暗、駭人的森林。就在最黑暗之處，突然間，樹叢中竄出一隻龐大的野獸，撲到他們面前。

【獅吼聲】

桃樂絲：「哦，瞧，那是一隻獅子，像馬一樣高大。哦，他打倒了稻草人。」

錫樵夫：「別擔心，我來把──嗯，哦，嗯，啊，啊……」

【獅吼聲和狗吠聲】

桃樂絲：「你敢咬托托！你應該感到羞愧，像你這樣大的野獸，還去咬一隻可憐的小狗狗！」

scary ： adj.
可怕的、驚駭的

in front of ：
在……之前

as big as ：
像……一樣大

knock ： v.
擊打

ashamed ： adj.
感到羞愧的

Cowardly Lion："I didn't bite him. And you hit me on my nose, on my nose."

Dorothy ："You tried to bite him. You are nothing but a big coward!"

Cowardly Lion ："I... I know it."

Dorothy ："Here, Mr. Scarecrow, I'll put you on your feet again."

＊膽小獅把稻草人和錫樵夫打倒在地。

膽小獅：「我沒有咬到牠。可是妳打到我的鼻子，
　　　　打到我的鼻子了。」

桃樂絲：「你想咬牠，你只是一個巨大的膽小鬼罷
　　　　了！」

膽小獅：「我……我知道我是個膽小鬼。」

桃樂絲：「來吧，稻草人先生，我扶你起來。」

coward ：n.
膽小的人、膽怯者

＊想到自己是個膽
　小鬼，膽小獅不
　禁悲從中來。

Scarecrow ："Thank you. Thank you very much."

Dorothy ："There you are, Tin Woodman, back on your feet."

The Tin Woodman ："Oh, thank you. Thank you."

Dorothy ："Mr. Lion, did you say you're a coward?"

Cowardly Lion ："Yes."

Dorothy ："But how can that be?"

Cowardly Lion ："Well, it's a mystery. I suppose I was born that way."

Scarecrow ："That isn't right. The King of Beasts shouldn't be a coward."

Cowardly Lion ："I... I know, it's my great sorrow."

The Tin Woodman ："Do you have a heart?"

Cowardly Lion ："Oh, yes, I'm sure I do."

稻草人：「謝謝妳，非常感謝。」

桃樂絲：「你也是，錫樵夫，我扶你起來。」

錫樵夫：「哦，謝謝妳，謝謝妳。」

桃樂絲：「獅子先生，你說你是個膽小鬼？」

膽小獅：「是的。」

桃樂絲：「可是，怎麼會這樣？」

膽小獅：「啊，這是個謎。我猜想我生下來就是這個樣子。」

稻草人：「這是不對的，萬獸之王不該是一個膽小鬼。」

膽小獅：「我……我知道，那是我最大的悲哀。」

錫樵夫：「你有心嗎？」

膽小獅：「哦，有的，我確定我有。」

mystery ： n.
神祕之事、謎

The King of
Beasts ：
萬獸之王

sorrow ： n.
悲傷、憂愁

The Tin Woodman："Well, you're lucky."

Scarecrow："Have you any brains?"

Cowardly Lion："I... I suppose so. I've never looked to see."

Scarecrow："I am going to the Great Oz to ask him to give me some."

Cowardly Lion："You are? But do you think the Great Oz could give me courage?"

Scarecrow："I should think so."

Cowardly Lion："Well, then, if you don't mind, I'll go with you, because my life is simply unbearable without a bit of courage."

錫樵夫：「啊，你真幸運。」

稻草人：「你有頭腦嗎？」

膽小獅：「我……我想有的。我從來沒有看過就是了。」

稻草人：「我要去找偉大的奧茲，請他給我一些頭腦。」

膽小獅：「你要去？你認為偉大的奧茲能夠給我勇氣嗎？」

稻草人：「我想會吧。」

膽小獅：「嗯，那麼，如果你們不介意的話，我想跟你們一塊兒去，因為少了勇氣，我的人生實在難以忍受。」

courage ： n.
勇氣、勇敢

simply ： adv.
完全地、徹底地

unbearable ： adj.
難以忍受的

The Emerald City
翡翠城

CD * 7

Narrator：So the little company set off once more on their journey to the Emerald City. At last, they came out of the forest into a beautiful country. Soon they saw a beautiful green glow in the sky. It was the Emerald City, a great gate studded with emeralds. Dorothy rang the bell.

【bell tolls】

旁白：就這樣，一夥人再度啓程前往翡翠城。終於他們走出了森林，來到美麗的鄉村。不久，他們看見天空一道漂亮的綠色光芒，那就是翡翠城，宏偉的大門鑲嵌著翡翠。桃樂絲搖響門鈴。

【鈴響聲】

* 沿著黃磚道一直走去，翡翠城就會出現在眼前。

company ： n.
夥伴、朋友、一行人

set off ：
出發

once more ：
又一次

at last ：
最後、終於

glow ： n.
光芒、光輝

studded with ：
鑲嵌著……

Narrator : Dorothy and her friends found themselves in a wonderful place. A big throne of green marble stood in the middle of the room, and on the throne was an enormous head. That's all. There was no body to support it, nor any arms or legs. The eyes were fixed on her. Suddenly, the mouth moved.

旁白：桃樂絲和她的朋友來到一個奇妙的地方，室內中央有一張巨大的綠色大理石寶座，寶座上方有一個碩大無比的頭。如此而已。沒有身體支撐它，也沒有手或腳。頭上的眼睛定定注視著桃樂絲，突然間，它的嘴巴動了。

＊寶座上方有一個碩大無比的頭。

throne ： n.
王座、寶座

marble ： n.
大理石

enormous ： adj.
碩大的、龐大的

fix on ：
凝視、注視

The Great Wizard of Oz

CD * 8

Oz："I am Oz, the Great and Terrible. Why do you seek me?"

Dorothy："Uh, uh, uh, I am Dorothy, the Small and Meek. These are my friends, and we have come to you for help."

Oz："Where did you get the silver slippers?"

Dorothy："I... I got them from the Wicked Witch of the East, when my house fell on her and killed her."

Oz："Where did you get the mark on your forehead?"

Dorothy："That's where the Good Witch of the North kissed me when she said good-bye."

Oz："What do you wish me to do?"

偉大的奧茲魔法師*

CD * 8

奧茲：「我是偉大而可怕的奧茲，妳找我有何事？」

桃樂絲：「嗯，嗯，嗯，我是渺小而溫順的桃樂絲。這幾位是我的朋友，我們前來求你幫忙。」

奧茲：「妳從哪弄來那雙銀鞋子？」

桃樂絲：「我……我從東方壞女巫那兒拿到的，我的房子壓在她身上，殺死了她。」

奧茲：「妳額頭上的記號又是從何而來？」

桃樂絲：「那是北方好女巫和我道別時，她吻我留下的記號。」

奧茲：「妳希望我做什麼呢？」

terrible ： adj.
可怕的

seek ： v.
尋覓、企求

meek ： adj.
溫和的、溫順的

forehead ： n.
前額、額頭

Dorothy："Please! Please send me back to Kansas, where my Aunt Em and Uncle Henry are waiting for me."

Oz："If you wish me to use my magic power to send you home again you must do something for me first."

Dorothy："What must I do?"

Oz："Kill the Wicked Witch of the West."

Dorothy："Kill? But I can't do that."

OZ："When you tell me she is dead, then I will send you back to Kansas, but not before."

Oz："Now, what do these others want?"

Scarecrow："I want some brains."

The Tin Woodman："I want a heart."

Cowardly Lion："And I want some courage."

Narrator：But Oz gave them all the same answer,

桃樂絲：「求求你！求求你送我回堪薩斯，艾姆嬸
　　　　嬸和亨利叔叔都在等著我。」

奧茲：「假如妳希望我用魔法送妳回家，妳要先為
　　　我做一些事。」

桃樂絲：「我該做什麼呢？」

奧茲：「殺死那個西方壞女巫。」

桃樂絲：「殺死？可是我不能夠那樣做。」

奧茲：「當妳告訴我說她已經掛了，到那時候，我
　　　就會送妳回堪薩斯。在此之前，免談。」

奧茲：「現在，其他幾位想要什麼呢？」

稻草人：「我要一些頭腦。」

錫樵夫：「我要一顆心。」

膽小獅：「還有，我要一些勇氣。」

旁白：可是，奧茲給他們每個人相同的答覆。

Oz ："Kill the Wicked Witch of the West. Now go, and do not ask to see me again until the Witch is dead."

奧茲：「殺死西方壞女巫。現在去吧，在女巫死亡之前，不要再來求見我。」

*一九三九年《綠野仙
蹤》電影上映時，推
出各項搭售商品。

*The Wicked Witch of the West

CD * 9

Dorothy ： "What shall we do now?"

Cowardly Lion ： "There's only one thing we can do. We must go to the land of the Winkies, seek out the Wicked Witch, and... and destroy her."

Narrator ： Now the Wicked Witch of the West had only one eye, but that was as powerful as a telescope, and could see everywhere. So as she sat in the door of her castle, she spied Dorothy and her friends coming into her land.

The Wicked Witch of the West ： "Hahahaha! I will destroy them all! Hahahaha!"

Narrator ： The Wicked Witch went to her cupboard, from it she took a Golden Cap, she put the cap on her head, and then she stood on her left foot and said, slowly,

西方壞女巫

CD＊9

桃樂絲：「我們現在該怎麼辦？」

膽小獅：「我們唯一能做的就是前往溫基人的國度，找到壞女巫，然後……消滅她。」

旁白：那西方壞女巫只有一隻眼睛，可是那隻眼睛像望遠鏡一樣厲害，看得見四面八方。所以她坐在城堡的門口，便發現桃樂絲和她的朋友闖入她的國境。

西方壞女巫：「哈哈哈哈！我要把他們全部都消滅！哈哈哈哈！」

旁白：壞女巫從櫥櫃裡拿出一頂金帽子，戴在頭上。然後她左腳獨立著，徐徐地說：

destroy：v.
毀滅、殺死

now：adj.
且說、卻說

telescope：n.
望遠鏡

spy：v.
祕密監看、發現

cupboard：n.
櫥、櫃

＊西方壞女巫戴上金帽
子，召喚飛天猴過來
供她差遣。

The Wicked Witch of the West："Ep-py, pep-py, kak-ky!"

Narrator：Then she stood on her right foot and said,

The Wicked Witch of the West："Hi-lo, ho-lo, hel-lo!"

Narrator：And after that, she stood on both feet and cried in a loud voice,

The Wicked Witch of the West："Ziz-zy, zuz-zy, zik!"

Narrator：The sky got dark, there was a low rumbling in the air and the rushing of many wings. And sudden-

＊飛天猴把膽小獅綑綁
起來，把他帶回西方
壞女巫的城堡裡。

rumbling：gerund
隆隆聲、隆隆地響

rushing：gerund
急衝
（此處動名詞當名詞
用）

西方壞女巫：「伊─霹、培─霹、卡─基！」

旁白：然後她右腳獨立著說：

西方壞女巫：「奚─羅，呵─囉，哈─囉！」

旁白：接著她並立著雙腳，大聲叫起來：

西方壞女巫：「西─靂，楚─靂，靂─克！」

旁白：天空變暗，一陣低沈的隆隆聲，許多翅膀急
衝而下。驀然間，一群飛天猴環繞著她。他

ly she was surrounded by the Winged Monkeys. Their leader said,

The Winged Monkeys："The Golden Cap gives you power over us three times. This is your third and last wish. What would you have us do for you, oh, Witch of the West?"

The Wicked Witch of the West："Go to the strangers in my land and destroy them all, except the Lion. I want him for my slave."

The Winged Monkeys："We must and we shall obey your commands."

Narrator： The Winged Monkeys flew away to the place where Dorothy was sleeping, while her friends stood watch. Some of the Monkeys seized the Tin Woodman.

The Tin Woodman："Get away from me, you beasts."

Narrator： Other Monkeys caught the Scarecrow and ripped him open.

們的領袖說：

飛天猴：「金帽子賦予妳三次使喚我們的權力。這
　　　　是妳的第三次，也是最後一次。我們如何為
　　　　妳效勞，哦，西方女巫？」

西方壞女巫：「到我的國境裡去搜索幾個陌生人，
　　　　　把他們全部都消滅，除了獅子以外。我要他
　　　　　做我的奴隸。」

飛天猴：「我們會遵從妳的命令。」

旁白：飛天猴飛到桃樂絲睡覺的地方，她的朋友站
　　　在一旁守護著。幾隻飛天猴抓住錫樵夫。

錫樵夫：「滾開，你們這群畜牲。」

旁白：其他的猴子抓住稻草人，把他扯裂開來。

wish：n.
願望

stranger：n.
陌生人

slave：n.
奴隸

obey：v.
服從

command：n.
命令

stand watch：
站哨、守衛

seize：v.
抓住

rip：v.
扯裂

Narrator ： The Lion they tied with ropes and took him to the Witch's castle. Then they flew back to capture Dorothy.

Dorothy ： "Now they are coming for us, Toto. Oh, dear, what will happen to us?"

The Winged Monkeys ： "Capture her and bind her with ropes. No, wait, wait, see that mark on her fore-head? That is the kiss of the Good Witch of the North. We dare not harm this little girl. All we can do is carry her to the castle and leave her there."

Narrator ： Which they did. They flew into the air and were soon out of sight.

旁白：至於獅子，飛天猴用繩子把他綑綁起來，帶到女巫的城堡裡。然後，他們飛回去抓桃樂絲。

桃樂絲：「現在牠們回來抓我們了。托托，哦，天啊，我們不知道會怎樣？」

飛天猴：「抓住她，用繩子把她綁起來。不，等等，看到她頭上的那個記號嗎？那是北方好女巫親吻留下的記號。我們不敢傷害這個小女孩，唯一能做的就是把她帶到城堡裡，把她留在那裡。」

旁白：他們這樣做了，然後飛向天空，不見蹤影。

capture：v.
擄獲

bind：v.
綑、綁

harm：v.
傷害

carry：v.
搬運、負載、抱著

castle：n.
城堡

out of sight：
消失、看不見

Water

CD * 10

Narrator ： The Wicked Witch was worried when she saw the mark on Dorothy's forehead, for she knew well that neither the Winged Monkeys, nor she, herself, dare hurt the girl in any way. But she thought,

The Wicked Witch of the West ： "I can still make her my slave. Come with me, and see that you do everything I tell you, and if you do not I will make an end of you, as I did of the Tin Woodman and the Scarecrow. Hahahaha!"

Dorothy ： "Yes, Ma'am."

The Wicked Witch of the West ： "And keep that nasty little dog away from me. Get away from me, I tell you. Get away from me!"

【sound of barking】

水

CD * 10

旁白：看到桃樂絲額頭上的記號，壞女巫有所顧慮，她知道無論是飛天猴或她自己都不敢用任何方式傷害這個女孩。然而她想道：

西方壞女巫：「我還是可以讓她作我的奴隸。跟我來，妳要聽我的吩咐行事。如果妳不聽從，我就讓妳完蛋，就像我對錫樵夫和稻草人所做的那樣。哈哈哈哈！」

桃樂絲：「是的，夫人。」

西方壞女巫：「叫那隻討厭的小狗滾開。滾開，我告訴你，滾開！」

【狗吠聲】

neither... nor：
既非……也非……

Ma'am：
（對女士的尊稱）
太太、小姐、夫人

keep... away：
防止、禁止

nasty：adj.
討厭的、難纏的

Dorothy："Toto, don't bite her. She'll do something bad to you."

Narrator：Ah, the Wicked Witch knew about Dorothy's silver slippers and the charm they carried. So she used her magic art to make Dorothy trip and fall, and one of the slippers came off.

The Wicked Witch of the West："Ah ha, I've got one of your shoes."

Dorothy："Give it back to me, give it back."

The Wicked Witch of the West："I will not. Now it's my shoe, not yours."

Dorothy："You are a wicked creature!"

The Wicked Witch of the West："Hahaha! Someday I'll get the other one from you, too. Hahaha!"

Dorothy："You make me so mad I am going to throw this pail of water on you."

桃樂絲：「托托，別咬她，她會對你使壞的。」

旁白：啊，壞女巫曉得桃樂絲的銀鞋子具有某種魔力，所以她運用魔法讓桃樂絲絆倒，摔了一跤，一只鞋子從她腳上掉下來。

西方壞女巫：「啊哈，我拿到妳的一只鞋子了。」

桃樂絲：「還給我，把鞋子還給我。」

西方壞女巫：「我不還，現在這只鞋子是我的，不是妳的了。」

桃樂絲：「妳這個壞東西！」

西方壞女巫：「哈哈哈！哪天我還要從妳那裡弄到另外一只鞋。哈哈哈！」

桃樂絲：「妳惹得我非常生氣，我要把這桶水潑在妳身上。」

trip ： v.
絆倒

creature ： n.
生物、人

mad ： adj.
發怒的

＊西方壞女巫氣忿忿地
說：「叫那隻討厭的
小狗滾開！」

The Wicked Witch of the West ："No! No! You mustn't, you don't dare do that."

Dorothy ："I most certainly do."

【sound of splashing】

splashing：gerund
潑灑、潑濺、潑水聲

＊一桶水潑在女巫身上，她就溶化了。

西方壞女巫：「不！不行！妳不可以這樣做，妳沒
膽子這樣做。」

桃樂絲：「我一定要這樣做。」

【潑水聲】

The Wicked Witch of the West："Oh, see what you've done! I'm melting away. In a minute I shall be gone."

Dorothy："Oh, oh, I'm very sorry, indeed."

The Wicked Witch of the West："Didn't you know water would be the end of me?"

Dorothy："No, no, of course not."

The Wicked Witch of the West："In a few more seconds I shall be all melted, and you will have the castle to yourself. Look out, look out — here I go!"

Dorothy："Toto, look. She's melted all away."

Dorothy："Cowardly Lion, Cowardly Lion, the Witch has melted away. We're free, we're free."

Cowardly Lion："Oh, I'm so glad, she scared me half to death."

西方壞女巫：「哦，看妳做的好事！我快溶化了，
　　　　　　再過一分鐘我就消失無蹤。」

桃樂絲：「哦，哦，我很抱歉，真的很抱歉。」

西方壞女巫：「難道妳不知道水會讓我完蛋嗎？」

melt：v.
溶化

桃樂絲：「哦，不知道，當然不知道。」

西方壞女巫：「再過幾秒鐘，我就全部溶化了，妳
　　　　　　可以把這座城堡據為己有。小心點，小心點
　　　　　　──我去了！」

桃樂絲：「托托，看，她已經溶化了。」

桃樂絲：「膽小獅，膽小獅，女巫已經溶化了。我
　　　　們自由了，我們自由了。」

膽小獅：「哦，我真高興，她把我嚇得半死。」

Free

CD * 11

Narrator ： After she set the Cowardly Lion loose, Dorothy called all the Winkies together. She asked them to help her find the Scarecrow and the Tin Woodman.

【sound of noise】

The Winkies ： "Of course, we will."

Narrator ： It took two days of searching, but the Winkies finally found them both. They pounded out the dents in the Tin Woodman, and stuffed the Scarecrow with new straw.

Scarecrow ： "Oh, thank you, everyone. I feel much better now."

Dorothy ： "That's wonderful, and the Wicked Witch is dead. Now we are ready to go back to Oz and make him keep his promise."

自由

CD ＊ 11

旁白：桃樂絲為膽小獅鬆綁後，她把全部的溫基人召集過來，請他們幫忙尋找稻草人和錫樵夫。

【嘈雜聲】

溫基人：「沒問題，我們願意幫妳忙。」

旁白：溫基人花了兩天的時間搜索，終於尋獲稻草人和錫樵夫。他們把錫樵夫身上的凹痕打平，在稻草人的裡面填塞新草。

稻草人：「哦，謝謝各位，我覺得好多了。」

桃樂絲：「太棒了，壞女巫已經掛了。現在我們要回到奧茲那兒，要他履行承諾。」

set...loose：
解開、放掉

pound：v.
重擊、猛打

dent：n.
凹痕

promise：n.
諾言、承諾

keep *one's*
promise：
履行承諾

＊他們把錫樵夫身上的凹痕敲平。

Narrator ： When they were preparing for their journey, the Scarecrow found the Golden Cap the Wicked Witch used to call the Winged Monkeys.

Scarecrow ： "Try it on, Dorothy. You never know, it might come in handy."

come in handy ：
派上用場

旁白：當他們正準備動身時，稻草人發現那頂壞女巫用來使喚飛天猴的金帽子。

稻草人：「戴看看吧，桃樂絲。誰知道哪天可以派上用場。」

＊他們在稻草人的裡面
填塞新的稻草。

Dorothy ："All right. Why, it fits perfectly, but we must be off to see the Wizard. Good-bye, Winkies."

The Winkies ："Good-bye, Dorothy... Good-bye, Dorothy..."

桃樂絲：「好吧。啊，戴上去剛剛好。我們得走了，去見魔法師。再見，溫基人。」

溫基人：「再見，桃樂絲！再見，桃樂絲！」

Promise

CD * 12

Narrator ： In two days our travelers were once again at the gate of the Emerald City. When they entered the Throne Room, the Throne was empty, but presently they heard a voice that seemed to come from somewhere near the top of the great dome.

Oz ： "I am Oz, the Great and Terrible. Why do you seek me?"

Dorothy ： "Great Wizard, we've done what you asked, now we want you to keep your promise."

Oz ： "Is the Wicked Witch dead?"

Dorothy ： "Yes, I melted her with a bucket of water."

Oz ： "Oh, dear me. Uh, uh, well, uh, come back tomorrow, for I must have time to think this over."

承諾

CD * 12

旁白：兩天後，這一隊旅行者再度來到翡翠城門口。當他們進入寶座廳時，寶座上空無一人，但他們立刻聽到一個聲音，似乎是從那巨大的圓屋頂附近傳下來的。

奧茲：「我是偉大而可怕的奧茲，妳為何來找我呢？」

桃樂絲：「偉大的魔法師，我們已經完成你的要求，現在我們要你履行承諾。」

奧茲：「壞女巫死啦？」

桃樂絲：「是的，我用一桶水把她澆溶了。」

奧茲：「天啊。嗯，好吧。嗯，明天再回到我這裡來，因為我必須有一點兒時間想一想。」

Throne Room：
寶座廳

empty： adj.
無人的、空著的

presently： adv.
不久、很快地

dome： n.
圓頂、圓屋頂

The Tin Woodman ："You've had plenty of time already."

Scarecrow ："We won't wait another minute."

Cowardly Lion ："Not another minute!"

【sound of roaring and barking】

錫樵夫：「你已經有充裕的時間了。」

稻草人：「我們一分鐘都不能再等了。」

膽小獅：「一分鐘也不行！」

【獅吼聲及狗叫聲】

plenty of：
充裕的

Humbug

CD ✳ 13

Narrator： There was a big screen standing in the corner of the Throne Room. The Lion's roar so startled Toto that he knocked over the screen. And standing in the spot the screen had hidden was a little old man, with a bald head and a wrinkled face.

Dorothy ："Who are you?"

Oz ："I'm Oz, the — the Great and — and Terrible? But don't hit me — please don't hit me — I'll do anything you want me to."

Dorothy ："But I thought Oz was a great big Head."

Oz ："Oh, you're wrong. You see, I've been making believe."

Dorothy ："Making believe? Aren't you a Great Wizard?"

冒牌貨、騙子 *＊
＊

CD ＊ 13

旁白：寶座廳裡立著一座大屏風。那獅子的吼叫聲
　　　嚇得托托撞倒了屏風，誰知屏風後面竟躲著
　　　一個小老頭，頭禿了，滿臉都是皺紋。

桃樂絲：「你是誰？」

奧茲：「我是偉——偉大的，可——可怕的奧茲？
　　　別打我——求求妳不要打我——妳要我做什
　　　麼都行。」

桃樂絲：「可是，我以為奧茲是一個大頭。」

奧茲：「哦，你們都錯了。瞧，我一直是偽裝的。」

桃樂絲：「偽裝的？你不是偉大的魔法師嗎？」

screen ： n.
屏風

startle ： v.
驚嚇

bald ： adj.
禿頭的

wrinkled ： adj.
有皺紋的

make believe ：
假裝、偽裝

＊奧茲承認：「一點兒也沒錯，我是個騙子！」

Oz ："Oh, shh, shh, shh, my dear, don't speak so loud, you'll be overheard — and I'll be ruined. See, I'm... I'm supposed to be a Great Wizard."

Dorothy ："Aren't you?"

Oz ："Oh, oh, not a bit of it, my dear; I'm just an ordinary man."

overhear ： v.
無意中聽到

ruin ： v.
毀滅

＊你不只是個普通人，
　你是個騙子！

奧茲：「哦，噓，噓，噓，我親愛的，輕聲點兒，
　　　不然會被偷聽了去──那樣我就毀了。瞧，
　　　我是──我本來應該是偉大的魔法師。」

桃樂絲：「你不是嗎？」

奧茲：「哦，哦，一點也不是，我親愛的；我不過
　　　是一個普通人。」

Scarecrow："You're more than that, you're a humbug."

Oz："Exactly so. Yes, uh, I am a humbug."

Scarecrow："You seem quite proud of yourself, you should be ashamed of what you've done."

Oz："Oh, I am — I certainly am. I have no magical powers at all, see, so I cannot keep my promises to you."

Dorothy："I think you're a very bad man."

Oz："Oh no, my dear, no, no, no, I'm really a very good man, I'm just a very bad Wizard."

Scarecrow："Mr. Oz, you are going to keep your promise to me, I want my brains."

Oz："You do? Hmm, well, well, uh — the rest of you leave, if I am to perform this magical thing, I must work in secret."

稻草人：「你不只是個普通人，你是個騙子。」

奧茲：「一點兒也沒錯。是的，嗯，我是個騙子。」

稻草人：「你似乎自我感覺良好，你應該為自己的
　　　　所作所為感到羞愧才是。」

奧茲：「哦，我是──我當然羞愧。我根本沒有魔
　　　　法，所以我無法履行對你們的承諾。」

桃樂絲：「我覺得你是個很壞的傢伙。」

奧茲：「哦，不，我親愛的，不，不，不，我其實
　　　　是個很好的人，不過是個很彆腳的魔法師。」

稻草人：「奧茲先生，你一定要履行對我的承諾，
　　　　我要我的頭腦。」

奧茲：「你要？嗯，好吧，好吧，嗯──你們其他
　　　　幾位暫時迴避一下，如果我要施展這個魔
　　　　法，一定要祕密進行。」

humbug：n.
騙子、冒牌貨

in secret：
祕密地

Brains, Heart, Courage
頭腦、心、勇氣

CD＊14

Narrator：When the others were gone, the old humbug took off the Scarecrow's head, and filled it full of bran flakes. As he put the head back on, he said,

Oz："Uh, hereafter, you will be a great man, for I've given you a big helping of bran-new brains."

Scarecrow："I'm feeling much brighter already."

旁白：當所有人離去後，老騙子取下稻草人的腦袋，然後塞滿了麥麩片。他把頭放回去，對稻草人說：

奧茲：「嗯，從此以後，你將成為一個偉大的人物，因為我給了你一大坨『全新麥麩片』頭腦。」

稻草人：「我覺得我變得聰明多了。」

*老騙子取下稻草人的
腦袋，塞滿了麥麩
片，再放回去。

bran flakes ： n.
麥麩片；一種穀類做
的食品（cereal），加
牛奶一起當早餐吃

hereafter ： adv.
從此以後

helping ： n.
（食物）一份

bran-new brains ：
這 裡 是 諧 音 字，
"bran-new"與「全新
的」（brand-new）音
類似，有幽默諷刺之
意

Narrator： Then Oz called in the Tin Woodman and gave him a new heart of red silk and sawdust. He gave the Lion a dishful of a greenish liquid that really wasn't very tasty, but he insisted the lion drink it. The Lion did, and went back to his friends happy as he could be.

Cowardly Lion ："Now I am full of courage."

【sound of roaring】

旁白：奧茲召喚錫樵夫進來，給他一顆新的心，是用紅絲綢和鋸屑做成的。他給獅子一碟淡綠色的汁液，雖然不太好喝，但他堅持要獅子喝下去。獅子照做了，開心得不得了地回到朋友那兒。

膽小獅：「現在我充滿了勇氣。」

【獅吼】

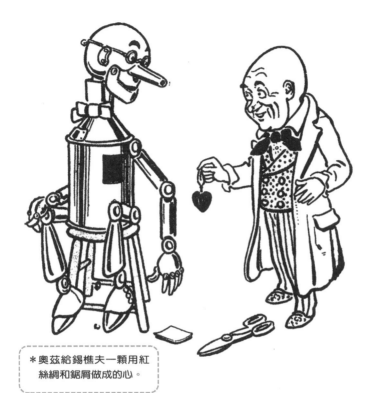

＊奧茲給錫樵夫一顆用紅
絲綢和鋸屑做成的心。

silk：n.
絲綢

sawdust：n.
鋸屑

dishful：n.
一碟的量、一盤的量

greenish：adj.
淡綠色的

liquid：n.
液體

tasty：adj.
美味可口的

insist：v.
堅持

Thinking Cap

CD * 15

Narrator ： When the Lion was gone, Oz said to himself,

Oz ："Well, I am glad I can make them happy, but it'll take
more than imagination to get Dorothy back to

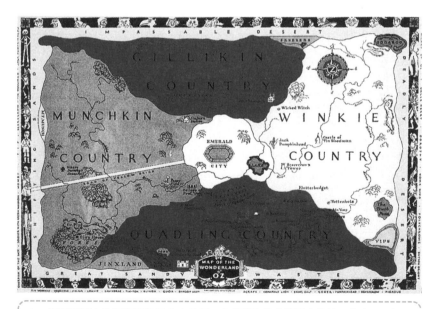

*一如堪薩斯在美國版圖的正中央位置，奧茲統治的翡翠城也位於正中央，不知是
作者故意安排，或純屬巧合？

思考帽

CD＊15

旁白：獅子離去後，奧茲自言自語：

奧茲：「啊呀，我真高興能讓他們快樂，可是要把
　　　桃樂絲送回堪薩斯，恐怕光有想像力是不夠

imagination：n.
想像力

＊奧茲煩惱著：「要
　把桃樂絲送回堪薩
　斯，恐怕光有想像
　力是不夠的。」

Kansas. I must put on my thinking cap. Ah, I have it!"

Narrator ： Next day, a very sad and unhappy Dorothy was called to the Throne Room. There she found Oz grinning from ear to ear.

Oz ： "Ah, well, young lady, I think I've found the way to get us out of this country."

Dorothy ： "Oh, that's wonderful. Oh, thank you, Mr. Oz, but you said 'us'. Are you going too?"

Oz ： "Oh, oh, absolutely. You see I'm tired of being such a humbug, and besides I want to be in the circus again."

Dorothy ： "I see, how are we going to get away?"

Oz ： "Oh, we'll make a balloon. See, that's how I got here and that's how we're going to get away."

的。我必須戴上我的思考帽。啊，我想到了！」

旁白：第二天，悶悶不樂的桃樂絲被召進寶座廳，她看到奧茲笑容滿面。

奧茲：「啊，這樣，小姑娘，我想我已經找到讓我們離開這個國度的方法。」

桃樂絲：「哦，太棒了。哦，謝謝你，奧茲先生，可是你說『我們』，你也要走嗎？」

奧茲：「哦，哦，鐵定的。妳看我已經厭倦了做一個騙子，此外，我想回到馬戲團裡。」

桃樂絲：「我知道了，但我們要怎麼離開呢？」

奧茲：「哦，我們要做一個熱氣球。妳知道嗎？當初我就是坐著熱氣球來到此地，所以我們也要坐熱氣球出去。」

unhappy ： adj.
不快樂的

grin ： v.
露齒而笑

young lady ：
年輕的小姐、小姑娘

absolutely ： adv.
絕對地、完全地

be tired of ：
厭倦的

circus ： n.
馬戲團

balloon ：
氣球；此處指可載人的「熱氣球」（hot air balloon）

Hot Air Balloon

CD * 16

Narrator ： So for the next three days, Dorothy and the Wizard sewed on a beautiful balloon. It was made out of green silk, and it was more than twenty feet high.

Oz ： "Oh, if I say so myself, it's a beauty! Now, now, now, we'll build a fire under it, and the hot air will fill it up. You people there, uh, tie this, uh, rope to the stake so the balloon doesn't fly away."

Dorothy ： "Mr. Oz, have you seen Toto, I can't go without him."

Oz ： "Uh, no, I haven't, but you'd better hurry up and find him, because the balloon is filling up fast, it's beginning to strain on the rope here. It's ready to go. I'll get in the basket. The Scarecrow, uh, uh, get Dorothy."

熱氣球

CD * 16

旁白：接下來三天，桃樂絲和魔法師一起縫製一個漂亮的熱氣球，以綠絲綢做成，超過二十英尺高。

奧茲：「哦，我說啊，這東西真漂亮！現在，現在，現在，我們在底下燒火，使熱氣灌滿。各位，嗯，幫忙綁住，唔，把繩子綁在柱子上，這樣氣球才不會飛走。」

桃樂絲：「奧茲先生，你有看見托托嗎？我不能丟下他離開。」

奧茲：「嗯，沒有，我沒看見。不過妳最好快點兒找到他，因為氣球充氣很快，繩子快要撐不住了。它快要升空了，我先跳進籃子裡。稻草人，唔，唔，快去叫桃樂絲。」

fill up：
充滿

tie：v.
綁、綑綁、繫縛

stake：n.
樁、柱

hurry up：
趕緊、快一點

strain：v.
用力拉、拉緊

basket：n.
籃子

Scarecrow ："Dorothy! Dorothy!"

Dorothy ："Here I am, I found Toto, I'm coming."

Oz ："Oh, oh, uh, the rope — uh, I'm going up......"

Dorothy ："Wait for me, wait for me."

Oz ："I can't, I'm on my way. Good-bye!"

【Dorothy sobs】

Dorothy ："Now I'll never get home!"

＊鮑姆創意十足，曾經
製作一批奧茲娃娃，
可惜叫好不叫座。

稻草人：「桃樂絲！桃樂絲！」

桃樂絲：「我在這，我找到托托，我來了。」

奧茲：「哦，哦，嗯，繩子──我要升空了……。」

桃樂絲：「等等我，等等我。」

奧茲：「我不能等了，上路啦，再會！」

【桃樂絲哭了】

桃樂絲：現在我永遠沒辦法回家了！

＊熱氣球升空，奧茲也跟著飛走了。

Glinda

CD * 17

Narrator：But the Scarecrow had an idea.

Scarecrow："You have the Golden Cap, why not call the Winged Monkeys? Have them take us to Glinda, the Good Witch of the South."

Dorothy："Oh, what a good idea. Your new brains are really working. Let's see now, first my left foot, 'Ep-py, pep-py, kak-ky!', and now my right foot, 'Hi-lo, ho-lo, hel-lo!', now both feet, 'Ziz-zy, zuz-zy, zik!'."

Narrator：And in no time at all, Dorothy and her friends were on their way to Glinda's Palace. She saw them at once.

Glinda："My friend, the Good Witch of the North told me you might pay a visit. How may I help you?"

葛琳達

CD ＊ 17

旁白：但是，稻草人有個主意。

稻草人：「妳有金帽子，為何不召喚飛天猴過來？
叫牠們帶我們去找南方好女巫葛琳達。」

桃樂絲：「哦，好主意。你的新腦袋的確管用。現
在讓我想想看，怎麼做才好。先左腳獨立
著，『伊─霹、培─霹、卡─基！』現在換
右腳，『奚─羅，呵─囉，哈─囉！』然後
兩隻腳並立，『西─靂，楚─靂，靂─克！』」

旁白：一瞬間，桃樂絲和她的朋友們已來到葛琳達
的皇宮，她馬上接見他們。

葛琳達：「我的朋友，北方好女巫已經跟我說過你
們會來造訪。我要怎麼幫你們呢？」

idea：n.
主意

work：v.
運轉

palace：n.
皇宮、宮殿

＊戴上金帽子，有三次
使喚飛天猴的權力。

Dorothy ："I so want to go to Kansas, Good Witch of the South. Aunt Em and Uncle Henry must be very worried about me."

Glinda ："That's the simplest thing in the world. You could've gone anytime you'd wished if only you had known."

＊飛天猴帶他們去找南方好女巫葛琳達。

could've：
CD 裡唸成 can've，
不太合一般文法

if only you had
known：
如果你早知道的話

桃樂絲：「我好想回堪薩斯，南方好女巫。艾姆嬸嬸和亨利叔叔一定擔心死我了。」

葛琳達：「那是世上最簡單不過的事了。假使妳知道的話，妳早就回去了。」

＊葛琳達說：「只要輕叩
鞋跟三下，它就會帶妳
到任何想去的地方。

Dorothy ： "Known what?"

Glinda ： "The secret of the silver slippers you are wearing. Click the heels together three times, and they will take you anywhere you wish to go."

Dorothy ： "Really?"

Glinda ： "Really. You say good-bye to your friends and one minute later you will be home."

click the heels ：
使鞋跟發出喀嗒聲

桃樂絲：「知道什麼？」

葛琳達：「妳穿的銀鞋子的祕密。只要輕叩鞋跟三下，它就會帶妳到任何妳想去的地方。」

桃樂絲：「真的嗎？」

葛琳達：「真的。妳跟朋友說再見吧，一分鐘後妳就可以回到家了。」

＊桃樂絲意識到，這是
她最後一次與好朋友
們道別。

Dorothy ："Home? Home in Kansas?"

Glinda ："Home in Kansas. So say good-bye."

Narrator ： Then, suddenly Dorothy realized that she was leaving her dear friends for the last time.

【Dorothy sobs】

realize ： v.
了解、完全知道

for the last time ：
最後一次

桃樂絲：「家？堪薩斯的家？」

葛琳達：「堪薩斯的家，所以說再見啦！」

旁白：然後，桃樂絲忽然意識到，這是她最後一次與好朋友們道別。

【桃樂絲哭了】

Going Home

CD * 18

Dorothy ："Good-bye, Scarecrow."

Scarecrow ："Good-bye, Dorothy."

Dorothy ："Good-bye, Tin Woodman."

Tin Woodman ："Good-bye, Dorothy."

Dorothy ："Good-bye, Cowardly Lion."

Cowardly Lion ："Good-bye, Dorothy."

Dorothy ："I love you all."

Narrator ： She hugged her friends, and then took Toto in her arms, and clapped the heels of her silver shoes together three times.

回家

CD ＊ 18

桃樂絲：「再見，稻草人。」

稻草人：「再見，桃樂絲。」

桃樂絲：「再見，錫樵夫。」

錫樵夫：「再見，桃樂絲。」

桃樂絲：「再見，膽小獅。」

膽小獅：「再見，桃樂絲。」

桃樂絲：「我愛你們每一位。」

旁白：她擁抱每一個朋友，然後把托托抱在她懷裡，輕叩三下銀鞋跟。

hug：v.
擁抱

clap：v.
碰撞

heel：n.
鞋跟

【sound of three claps】

Dorothy ： "Take me home to Aunt Em!"

Dorothy ： "Oh, where am I?"

Aunt Em ： "Dorothy! Dorothy!"

Dorothy ： "Aunt Em."

Aunt Em ： "We've been looking all over for you. Where in the world did you come from?"

Dorothy ： "I came from the Land of Oz, Aunt Em, and I'm so glad to be home again!"

【輕叩三下鞋跟】

桃樂絲：「帶我回家，回到艾姆嬸嬸那裡！」

桃樂絲：「哦，我在哪？」

艾姆嬸嬸：「桃樂絲！桃樂絲！」

glad：adj.
歡喜的、高興的

桃樂絲：「艾姆嬸嬸。」

艾姆嬸嬸：「我們到處找妳，妳究竟從哪兒跑回來
　　　　　的？」

桃樂絲：「我從奧茲的國度回來的，艾姆嬸嬸，回
　　　　　家真好！」

＊回家真好！

中英有聲解說

CD * 19

Key words ：

Dorothy ran after him. ：桃樂絲跑過去追牠。

I'm so sleepy. ：我好睏、我好想睡覺。

adventure ：冒險、歷險記。

Kansas ：堪薩斯州。

prairie ：草原。

farmer ：農夫。

cellar ：地窖。

whirlwind ：旋風。

cyclone ：龍捲風。

wiggle ：扭動、擺脫。

CD * 20

shriek ：哀嚎、尖叫。

balloon ：氣球。

get over ：克服。

fright ：驚駭。

fast asleep ：入睡、睡著。

I thought there were no more witches. ：我以為已經沒有女巫了。

scream ：尖叫。

grateful ：感激的。

wizard ：魔法師、巫師。

emerald ：翡翠。

CD＊21

anxious ：渴望的、急切的、擔心的。

surround ：圍繞。

sob ：抽噎聲、啜泣聲。

pointed ：尖的。

chalk ：粉筆。

journey ：旅程、旅行。

possess ：擁有。

I don't want people to call me a fool. ：我不想讓大家叫我蠢貨。

set out ：啟程。

pole ：竿、柱、桿。

CD＊22

cornfield ：玉米田。

straw ：稻草。

wink ：眨眼示意。

nod ：點頭。

oblige ：感激、感謝。

bite ：咬。

match ：火柴。

I've been groaning for more than a year. ：我呻吟一年多了。

trudge ：長途跋涉。

cottage ：小屋。

CD＊23

shiny ：發光的。

groan ：呻吟。

jaw ：顎。

joint ：關節、接合處。

squirt ：噴出、射出。

tinsmith ：錫匠。

breast ：胸部。

He is as big as a horse. ：他像馬一樣高大。

The King of Beasts shouldn't be a coward.：萬獸之王不該
  是一個膽小鬼。

knock ：擊打。

CD＊24

ashamed ：感到羞愧的。

coward ：膽小的人、膽怯者。

The King of Beasts ：萬獸之王。

sorrow ：悲傷、不幸。

courage ：勇氣、勇敢。

unbearable ：難以忍受的。

There was no body to support it, nor any arms or legs.：沒
  有身體支撐它，也沒有手或腳。

glow ：發光。

studded with ：鑲嵌著。

CD＊25

throne ：王座、寶座。

marble ：大理石。

enormous ：碩大的、龐大的。

terrible ：可怕的。

telescope ：望遠鏡。

cupboard ：櫥、櫃。

stranger ：陌生人。

slave ：奴隸。

seize ：抓住。

castle ：城堡。

CD * 26

out of sight ：消失、看不見。

trip ：絆倒。

melt ：溶化。

I feel much better now. ：我覺得好多了。

dent ：凹痕。

promise ：諾言、承諾。

We want you to keep your promise. ：我們要你履行承諾。

empty ：無人的、空著的。

dome ：圓頂、圓屋頂。

screen ：屏風。

CD * 27

startle ：吃驚、驚跳。

bald ：禿頭的。

wrinkle ：皺紋。

making believe ：假裝、偽裝。

overhear ：無意中聽到。

ruin ：毀滅。

humbug ：騙子、冒牌貨。

silk ：絲綢。

sawdust ：鋸屑。

greenish ：呈綠色的。

CD ＊28

liquid ：液體。

tasty ：可口的。

imagination ：想像力。

circus ：馬戲團。

stake ：樁、柱。

hurry up ：趕緊、快一點。

strain ：用力拉、拉緊。

basket ：籃。

If only you had known ：如果妳早知道就好了。

hug ：擁抱。

heel ：鞋跟。

綠野仙蹤

　　這部由經典名著改編的有聲書，一共有 18 段。

　　每次把 CD 從頭聽到尾，當然更可以躺著聽。最後做克漏字，把括弧內遺漏的單字或片語（有的括弧內不只一個字）寫下，看看自己的聽力程度如何。解答附在每一組內文之後。

　　記住，先聽十遍，再做克漏字。

　　一開始不要先看原文，以免寵壞了耳朵，它就不管用了。

　　在後半部，由兩位中美老師仔細唸出單字及片語，覆述重要的句子。尤其是單字以清晰的美語發音，並拼出字母，可幫助你輕鬆記憶單字及片語。只要多聽幾遍，你將會驚訝地發現，原來英語可以聽聽就會。

　　聽力小祕訣：先聽十遍，再做克漏字。即使不能完全聽懂，也要讓耳朵熟悉英語的聲音與腔調。

　　這部《綠野仙蹤》有聲書是一齣舞台劇，充滿戲劇和音效的臨場感。剛開始你也許不太適應，但只要多聽幾遍，耳朵熟能生巧，漸漸就能融會貫通。

　　學英語要像吃自助餐，不要老吃同一道菜，最好是各色好菜搭配著吃，這樣才不會吃膩。所以，建議你把家裡的幾套 CD 有聲書拿出來，替換著聽，一來避免聽膩了，二來英語更容易觸類旁通，聽力越練越好，會話也跟著進步，然後能提筆寫作。

　　倘若你的聽力不佳，聽不懂別人說的話，那要如何回答呢？恐怕是「答非所問」。所以要先會聽，就會說，也會寫。

　　聽有聲書，你會發現，學英語是多麼有趣的過程。你並不需要認識每一個單字，也不必完全聽懂所有的句子，就能輕鬆享受聽故事的樂趣。

＊《綠野仙蹤》作者鮑姆
伏案寫作時的神情。

龍捲風

第一組聽力測驗： CD ＊ 1

旁白：This is the story about the （1.　　　　　） of a little girl （2.　　　　　） Dorothy. She lived in the （3.　　　　　） of the great great Kansas （4.　　　　　） with her Aunt Em and Uncle Henry, who was a （5.　　　　　） . Their house was one room with a small （6.　　　　　） in the ground （7.　　　　　） the floor, which was a cyclone （8.　　　　　） , where the family could be safe in case one of those great （9.　　　　　） arose.

旁白：Aunt Em and Uncle Henry never laughed, but Dorothy did, and her little black dog Toto. Toto played all day and Dorothy played with him. Today, however, they weren't playing. Uncle Henry looked （10.　　　　　） at the sky, which was greyer than usual. There was a low （11.　　　　　） of wind.

亨利叔叔："Cyclone's coming in. I'll go look after the
（12.   ）. You and Dorothy get in the cellar there."

旁白： But Toto（13.   ） out of Dorothy's arms
and ran to（14.   ） under the big bed.
Dorothy ran after him.

桃樂絲："Toto, come here."

旁白： Oh, Dorothy was too late. There was a great
（15.   ） from the wind and the house
（16.   ） so hard that Dorothy fell down on
the floor.

艾姆嬸嬸："Dorothy! Dorothy!"

旁白： And then, a（17.   ） thing happened.
The house rose slowly in the air.

桃 樂 絲 ： "Toto, it's like we're going up in a
（18.   ）."

旁白： Slowly Dorothy（19.   ） her（ 20.   ）
and after a while she crawled over to her bed.

桃樂絲："Oh, Toto, I'm so（21.   ）."

旁白：And soon Dorothy and her little dog were
　　（22.　　　　）.

✻ 第一組測驗解答：

1. adventures 2. named 3. midst 4. prairie

5. farmer 6. hole 7. beneath 8. cellar 9. whirlwinds

10. anxiously 11. wail 12. cattle 13. wiggled

14. hide 15. shriek 16. shook 17. strange 18. balloon

19. got over 20. fright 21. sleepy 22. fast asleep

聽 力 測 驗

芒虛金

第二組聽力測驗：　　　　　　　　　　　　CD ✻ 2

哀嚎聲："Ahhhhh!"

桃樂絲："Toto, what was that? It was a（1.　　　　）!
　　　　Where are we?"

桃樂絲："We've landed（2.　　　　）. Let's look out
　　　　the window. Oh, look, it's so beautiful, green trees

and（3.　　　　　）and（4.　　　　　）and
（5.　　　　　）and butterflies and birds. Toto,
look!"

桃樂絲："There is a little old woman. She is coming up
　　　　here. Let's go out and say hello to her Toto, then
　　　　we can（6.　　　　　）where we are."

桃樂絲："Come on Toto."

桃樂絲："Helloooo."

北方好女巫："You are welcome, most noble Sorceress, to
　　　　the land of the Munchkins. We are so
　　　　（7.　　　　　）to you for having killed the
　　　　Wicked Witch of the East."

桃樂絲："Killed? I haven't killed（8.　　　　　）."

北方好女巫："Hahahaha! Oh, your house（9.　　　　）
　　　　her. Hahahaha!"

桃樂絲："That's what we（10.　　　　　），Toto."

北方好女巫："See her two（11.　　　　　）shoes?
　　　　There, she's gone."

桃樂絲："But who was she?"

北方好女巫："She was the Wicked Witch of the East. I'm
　　　　a witch too."

桃樂絲："You are?"

北方好女巫："Oh, yes,（12.　　　　　）. But I am the Good Witch of the North, and the people love me. Now there is only one Wicked Witch （13.　　　　　）, the Wicked Witch of the West."

桃樂絲："But I thought there were（14.　　　　）witches."

北方好女巫："Oh yes, oh yes, we still have witches here, and（15.　　　　　）."

桃樂絲："Who are the wizards?"

北方好女巫："Oz himself is the Great Wizard. He is more （16.　　　　　）than all the rest of us together. He lives in the City of Emeralds."

桃樂絲："Well, Mrs. Good Witch of the North, I am anxious to get back to my Aunt and Uncle. I know they're worried about me. Can you help me find my way?"

北方好女巫："I am afraid not, my dear. You see, a great desert（17.　　　　　）the whole Land of Oz. So I'm afraid you're going to have to live here with us."

桃樂絲："Oh, then I'll never get home again. Oh, Toto, we'll never get home again."

＊第二組測驗解答：

1. scream 2. somewhere 3. apples 4. pears

5. hills 6. find out 7. grateful 8. anybody 9. fell on

10. heard 11. silver 12. indeed 13. left

14. no more 15. wizards 16. powerful 17. surrounds

聽力測驗

黃磚道

第三組聽力測驗：   CD ＊ 3

旁白：As Dorothy（1.　　　　　）, the little old woman took off her（2.　　　　）cap and bounced the point on the end of her （3.　　　　）. At once the cap changed to a （4.　　　　）on which was written in big, white（5.　　　　）:

桃樂絲："LET DOROTHY GO TO THE CITY OF EMER-
ALDS."

桃樂絲："What does that mean?"

北方好女巫："Follow the yellow（6.　　　　　）road. It
is a long（7.　　　　　）and sometimes very
（8.　　　　　）. But if you get to the City of
Emeralds, the Great Oz may be able to help you."

桃樂絲："Won't you please go with me? I'm afraid."

北方好女巫："Oh, no, I cannot do that. But I will
（9.　　　　　）your（10.　　　　　）with my
kiss. No one would ever dare to（11.　　　　　）
a person who has been kissed by the Witch of the
North. Here."

桃樂絲："Thank you."

桃樂絲："Are there any other good witches
（12.　　　　　）you?"

北方好女巫："Oh, yes, there is Glinda, the Good Witch of
the South. She is the most powerful of us all,
（13.　　　　　）Oz. But she lives a long way
（14.　　　　　）. Well, now, I must leave you. I
（15.　　　　　）you to put on those silver slip-

pers. I am told they（16.　　　　）a powerful charm, perhaps they can do you good. Good-bye, my dear."

> ✱第三組測驗解答：

1. sobbed 2. pointed 3. nose 4. blackboard 5. chalk 6. brick 7. journey 8. dangerous 9. mark 10. brow 11. injure 12. besides 13. except 14. off 15. advise 16. possess

聽 力 測 驗

稻草人

第四組聽力測驗： CD ✱ 4

旁白：Dorothy（1.　　　　　）the silver slippers which（2.　　　　）perfectly. Then she and Toto set out（3.　　　　　）a long journey to the City of Emeralds and the Great Wizard of Oz （4.　　　　　）the yellow brick road. After she'd walked（5.　　　）miles, she saw a Scarecrow high on a（6.　　　）in a （7.　　　）. His blue suit was（8.　　　） with（9.　　　）. Dorothy looked into his （10.　　　）face and then（11.　　　）, she said to Toto,

桃樂絲："Toto, that Scarecrow（12.　　　）at me. And look, he is（13.　　　）. I am going over and say hello to him."

稻草人："Good day."

桃樂絲："Did you speak?"

稻草人："Certainly, how do you do?"

桃樂絲："Huh, pretty well, thank you. How do you do?"

稻草人："I'm not feeling well. This pole is （14.　　　）my back. If you will please take me off the pole I shall be greatly（15.　　　） to you."

桃樂絲："All right."

稻草人："Oh, thank you very much. Without that pole up my back, I feel like a new man. Who are you? And where are you going?"

桃樂絲："My name is Dorothy, and I am going to the (16.　　　　) to ask the Great Oz to send me back to Kansas."

稻草人："Where is the Emerald City?"

桃樂絲："Don't you know?"

稻草人："No, indeed. I don't know anything. You see, I am stuffed with straw, so I have no brains (17.　　　　) ."

桃樂絲："Oh, I'm awfully sorry for you."

稻草人："Do you think, if I go to the Emerald City with you, that the Great Oz would give me some (18.　　　　) ?"

桃樂絲："I don't know, but I'd be happy to have you come with me."

稻草人："I don't mind being stuffed with straw, because I can't get (19.　　　　) . But I don't want people to call me a (20.　　　　) , and with no brains, how am I ever to know anything?"

桃樂絲："I understand how you feel. Well, come along and we'll see what Oz can do for you."

稻草人："Thank you."

托托："woof, woof, woof."

桃樂絲："Toto, stop that. Mr. Scarecrow, don't mind him, he never（21.　　　　　）."

稻草人："Oh, I'm not afraid. There is only one thing in the world I'm afraid of."

桃樂絲："What is that?"

稻草人："A（22.　　　　　）."

＊第四組測驗解答：

1. put on 2. fit 3. on 4. along 5. several 6. pole

7. cornfield 8. stuffed 9. straw 10. painted

11. in surprise 12. winked 13. nodding 14. stuck up

15. obliged 16. Emerald City 17. at all 18. brains

19. hurt 20. fool 21. bites 22. lighted match

錫樵夫

第五組聽力測驗：　　　　　　　　　　　　　　　**CD ＊ 5**

旁白：So the three of them, Dorothy, Toto and the Scarecrow（1.　　　　）down the yellow brick road（2.　　　　）. After a while, they came to a great（3.　　　　）. They picked their way along（4.　　　　）, in a（5.　　　　）, they saw a little（6.　　　　）. But there seemed to be no one（7.　　　　）.

桃樂絲："What was that?"

桃樂絲："There it is again. What on earth is that? It sounds like（8.　　　　）in terrible trouble."

稻草人："It does indeed."

桃樂絲："Come on, let's see if we can help. Come on, Toto."

稻草人："I see something（9.　　　　）over there."

桃 樂 絲："Yes, I see it too. It looks like a man（10.　　　　）tin."

桃樂絲："Excuse me, sir. Did you（11.　　　　）?"

錫樵夫："Yes, I did. I've been groaning for more than a year but nobody's ever（12.　　　　）me, because my（13.　　　　）are rusted shut."

桃樂絲："How can I help you?"

錫樵夫："Get an oil can and oil my（14.　　　　）. There's an oil can by my cottage."

旁白：Dorothy ran back to the cottage, got the oil can, and（15.　　　　）oil on the Tin Woodman's joints.

錫樵夫："Oh, thank you. Oh, thank you, again and again. I might have（16.　　　　）there for always if you had not come along."

旁白：Dorothy explained that they were on their way to see the Great Wizard of Oz. The Tin Woodman （17.　　　　）to think deeply for（18.　　　　）, and then he said,

錫樵夫："Do you, do you（19.　　　　）Oz could give me a heart?"

桃樂絲："Why, I guess so. Don't you have a heart?"

錫樵夫："No. You see, the（20.　　　　）forgot to put

a heart in my（21.　　　　　）, and I truly miss it. So, if you'll allow me to（22.　　　　　）your party, I'll also go to the Emerald City, and I'll ask Oz for a heart."

稲草人："Come on along."

*第五組測驗解答：

1. trudged 2. together 3. forest 4. until 5. clearing

6. cottage 7. around 8. somebody's 9. shiny

10. made of 11. groan 12. heard 13. jaws 14. joints

15. squirted 16. stood 17. appeared 18. a moment

19. suppose 20. tinsmith 21. breast 22. join

聽力測驗

膽小獅

第六組聽力測驗： CD * 6

旁白：The yellow brick road（1.　　　　　）through a dark and（2.　　　　　）forest. And just where it was darkest, suddenly a great (3.   ) leaped out of the trees in front of them.

桃樂絲："Oh, look, it's a lion, and he is (4.   ) a horse. Oh, he's (5.   ) over the Scarecrow."

錫樵夫："Don't worry, I'll get, uh, uh, uh, ooh, ooh..."

桃樂絲："Don't you dare (6.   ) Toto! You ought to be (7.   ) of yourself, a big beast like you biting a (8.   ) little dog!"

膽小獅："I didn't bite him. And you (9.   ) me on my (10.   ), on my nose."

桃樂絲："You tried to bite him. You are nothing but a big (11.   ) !"

膽小獅："I... I know it."

桃樂絲："Here, Mr. Scarecrow, I'll put you on your (12.   ) again."

稻草人："Thank you. Thank you very much."

桃樂絲："There you are, Tin Woodman, back on your feet."

錫樵夫："Oh, thank you. Thank you."

桃樂絲："Mr. Lion, did you say you're a coward?"

膽小獅："Yes."

桃樂絲："But how can that be?"

膽小獅："Well, it's a（13.　　　　　）. I suppose I was born that way."

稻草人："That isn't right. The King of Beasts（14.　　　　　）be a coward."

膽小獅："I... I know, it's my great（15.　　　　　）."

錫樵夫："Do you have a heart?"

膽小獅："Oh, yes, I'm sure I do."

錫樵夫："Well, you're lucky."

稻草人："Have you any brains?"

膽小獅："I... I suppose so. I've never looked to see."

稻草人："I am going to the Great Oz to ask him to give me some."

膽小獅："You are? But do you think the Great Oz could give me（16.　　　　　）?"

稻草人："I should think so."

膽小獅："Well, then, if you don't mind, I'll go with you, because my life is simply（17.　　　　　）without a bit of courage."

＊第六組測驗解答：

1. led 2. scary 3. beast 4. as big as 5. knocked

6. bite 7. ashamed 8. poor 9. hit 10. nose

11. coward 12. feet 13. mystery 14. shouldn't

15. sorrow 16. courage 17. unbearable

聽力測驗

＊　　＊　　＊　　**翡翠城**

第七組聽力測驗：　　　　　　　　　　　　　　CD ＊ 7

旁　白 ： So the little (1.　　　　　) set off

(2.　　　　　) on their journey to the Emerald

City. At last, they came out of the forest into a

beautiful country. (3.　　　　　) they saw a

beautiful green (4.　　　　　) in the sky. It was

the Emerald City, a great gate (5.　　　　　)

with emeralds. Dorothy rang the（6.　　　　）.

旁白：Dorothy and her friends found（7.　　　　）

in a wonderful（8.　　　　）. A big throne of

green（9.　　　　）stood in the（10.　　　　）

of the room, and on the（11.　　　　）was an

（12.　　　　）head. That's all. There was no

body to（13.　　　　）it, nor any arms or legs.

The eyes were（14.　　　　）her. Suddenly,

the（15.　　　　）moved.

*第七組測驗解答：

1. company 2. once more 3. Soon 4. glow

5. studded 6. bell 7. themselves 8. place

9. marble 10. middle 11. throne 12. enormous

13. support 14. fixed on 15. mouth

偉大的奧茲魔法師

第八組聽力測驗：   CD * 8

奧茲："I am Oz, the Great and Terrible. Why do you （1.   ) me?"

桃樂絲："Uh, uh, uh, I am Dorothy, the Small and （2.   ). These are my friends, and we have come to you for help."

奧茲："Where did you get the silver slippers?"

桃樂絲："I... I got them from the Wicked Witch of the （3.   ), when my house (4.   ) her and killed her."

奧茲："Where did you get the mark on your （5.   )?"

桃樂絲："That's where the Good Witch of the （6.   ) kissed me when she said good-bye."

奧茲："What do you （7.   ) me to do?"

桃樂絲："Please! Please send me back to Kansas, where

my Aunt Em and Uncle Henry are（8.　　　）

me."

奧茲：“If you wish me to use my（9.　　　）

power to send you home again you must do some-

thing for me（10.　　　）."

桃樂絲：“What must I do?"

奧茲：“Kill the Wicked Witch of the（11.　　　　）."

桃樂絲：“Kill? But I can't do that."

奧茲：“When you tell me she is（12.　　　）, then I

will send you back to Kansas, but not

（13.　　　）."

奧茲：“Now, what do these（14.　　　）want?"

稻草人：“I want some brains."

錫樵夫：“I want a heart."

膽小獅：“And I want some courage."

旁白： But Oz gave them all the（15.　　　）

answer,

奧茲：“Kill the Wicked Witch of the West. Now go, and do

not ask to see me again until the Witch is dead."

＊第八組測驗解答：

1. seek 2. Meek 3. East 4. fell on 5. forehead

6. North 7. wish 8. waiting for 9. magic 10. first

11. West 12. dead 13. before 14. others 15. same

聽力測驗

西方壞女巫

第九組聽力測驗： CD ＊ 9

桃樂絲："What shall we do now?"

膽小獅："There's only one thing we can do. We must go to the land of the Winkies, seek out the Wicked Witch, and... and（1.　　　　　）her."

旁白：Now the Wicked Witch of the West had only one （2.　　　　　）, but that was as powerful as a （3.　　　　　）, and could see（4.　　　　　）. So as she sat in the door of her（5.　　　　　）, she spied Dorothy and her friends coming into her land.

西方壞女巫："Hahahaha! I will destroy them all! Hahahaha!"

旁白： The Wicked Witch went to her（6.　　　　），from it she took a Golden Cap, she put the（7.　　　　） on her head, and then she stood on her（8.　　　　） and said, slowly,

西方壞女巫："Ep-py, pep-py, kak-ky!"

旁白： Then she stood on her（9.　　　　） and said,

西方壞女巫："Hi-lo, ho-lo, hel-lo!"

旁白： And after that, she stood on（10.　　　　） feet and cried in a（11.　　　　） voice,

西方壞女巫："Ziz-zy, zuz-zy, zik!"

旁白： The sky got dark, there was a low（12.　　　　） in the air and the rushing of many（13.　　　　）. And suddenly she was（14.　　　　） by the Winged Monkeys. Their（15.　　　　） said,

飛天猴： "The Golden Cap gives you power（16.　　　　） us three times. This is your（17.　　　　） wish. What would you have us do for you, oh, Witch of the West?"

西方壞女巫："Go to the（18.　　　　　）in my land and destroy them all, except the Lion. I want him for my （19.　　　　　）."

飛天猴："We must and we shall（20.　　　　　）your （21.　　　　　）."

旁白：The Winged Monkeys（22.　　　　　）to the place where Dorothy was sleeping, while her friends stood（23.　　　　　）. Some of the Monkeys（24.　　　　　）the Tin Woodman.

錫樵夫："Get away from me, you beasts."

旁白：Other Monkeys（25.　　　　　）the Scarecrow and（26.　　　　　）him open.

旁白：The Lion they tied with（27.　　　　　）and took him to the Witch's castle. Then they flew back to （28.　　　　　）Dorothy.

桃樂絲："Now they are coming for us, Toto. Oh, dear, what will happen to us?"

飛天猴："Capture her and（29.　　　　　）her with ropes. No, wait, wait, see that mark on her fore- head? That is the kiss of the Good Witch of the

North. We dare not（30.　　　　） this little girl.
All we can do is（31.　　　　） her to the castle
and leave her there."

旁白：Which they did. They flew into the air and were
　　　soon（32.　　　　）.

＊第九組測驗解答：

1. destroy 2. eye 3. telescope 4. everywhere

5. castle 6. cupboard 7. cap 8. left foot 9. right foot

10. both 11. loud 12. rumbling 13. wings

14. surrounded 15. leader 16. over 17. third and last

18. strangers 19. slave 20. obey 21. commands

22. flew away 23. watch 24. seized 25. caught

26. ripped 27. ropes 28. capture 29. bind 30. harm

31. carry 32. out of sight

水

第十組聽力測驗：　　　　　　　　　　CD * 10

旁白：The Wicked Witch was worried when she saw the mark on Dorothy's forehead, for she knew well that （1.　　　　　） the Winged Monkeys, nor she, herself, dare hurt the girl in any way. But she thought,

西方壞女巫："I can still make her my slave. Come with me, and see that you do everything I tell you, and if you do not I will make an end of you, as I did of the Tin Woodman and the Scarecrow. Hahahaha!"

桃樂絲："Yes, Ma'am."

西方壞女巫："And keep that （2.　　　　　） little dog away from me. Get away from me, I tell you. Get away from me."

桃樂絲："Toto, don't bite her. She'll do something bad to you."

旁白：Ah, the Wicked Witch knew about Dorothy's silver

slippers and the charm they carried. So she used her magic art to make Dorothy（3.　　　） and（4.　　　）, and one of the slippers came off.

西方壞女巫："Ah ha, I've got one of your shoes."

桃樂絲："Give it back to me, give it back."

西方壞女巫："I will not. Now it's my shoe, not（5.　　　）."

桃樂絲："You are a wicked（6.　　　）!"

西方壞女巫："Hahaha! Someday I'll get the other one from you, too. Hahaha!"

桃樂絲："You make me so（7.　　　）I am going to（8.　　　）this（9.　　　）of water on you."

西方壞女巫："No! No! You mustn't, you don't dare do that."

桃樂絲："I most（10.　　　）do."

西方壞女巫："Oh, see what you've done! I'm（11.　　　）away. In a minute I shall be gone."

桃樂絲："Oh, oh, I'm very sorry,（12.　　　）."

西方壞女巫："Didn't you know water would be
（13.　　　　）me?"

桃樂絲："No, no, of course not."

西方壞女巫："In a few more（14.　　　　）I shall be
all melted, and you will have the castle to
（15.　　　　）. Look out, look out — here I go!"

桃樂絲："Toto, look. She's（16.　　　　）all away."

桃樂絲："Cowardly Lion, Cowardly Lion, the Witch has
melted away. We're free, we're free."

膽 小 獅 ："Oh, I'm so glad, she scared me
（17.　　　　）to death."

＊第十組測驗解答：

1. neither 2. nasty 3. trip 4. fall 5. yours

6. creature 7. mad 8. throw 9. pail 10. certainly

11. melting 12. indeed 13. the end of 14. seconds

15. yourself 16. melted 17. half

自由

第十一組聽力測驗： CD ＊ 11

旁白： After she（1. 　　　　　） the Cowardly Lion
（2. 　　　　　）, Dorothy called all the Winkies
（3. 　　　　　）. She asked them to help her find
the Scarecrow and the Tin Woodman.

The Winkies： "Of course, we will."

旁白： It took two days of（4. 　　　　　）, but the
Winkies finally found them（5. 　　　　　）.
They pounded out the（6. 　　　　　）in the Tin
Woodman, and stuffed the Scarecrow with new
（7. 　　　　　）.

稻草人： "Oh, thank you, everyone. I feel much better
now."

桃樂絲： "That's wonderful, and the Wicked Witch is dead.
Now we are ready to go back to Oz and make him
（8. 　　　　　） his（9. 　　　　　）."

旁白：When they were preparing for their journey, the Scarecrow found the Golden Cap the Wicked Witch （10.　　　　　） to call the Winged Monkeys.

稻草人："Try it on, Dorothy. You never know, it might come （11.　　　　　） ."

桃樂絲："All right. Why, it （12.　　　　　） perfectly, but we must be （13.　　　　） to see the Wizard. Good-bye, Winkies."

溫基人："Good-bye, Dorothy! Good-bye, Dorothy!"

＊第十一組測驗解答：

1. set　2. loose　3. together　4. searching　5. both

6. dents　7. straw　8. keep　9. promise　10. used

11. in handy　12. fits　13. off

聽力測驗

承諾

第十二組聽力測驗： CD ＊ 12

旁白： In two days our （1.　　　　） were once again at the （2.　　　　） of the Emerald City. When they entered the Throne Room, the Throne was （3.　　　　）, but presently they heard a Voice that seemed to come from somewhere near the top of the great （4.　　　　）.

奧茲： "I am Oz, the Great and Terrible. Why do you seek me?"

桃樂絲： "Great Wizard, we've （5.　　　　） what you asked, now we want you to keep your promise."

奧茲： "Is the Wicked Witch dead?"

桃樂絲： "Yes, I melted her with a （6.　　　　） of water."

奧茲： "Oh, dear me. Uh, uh, well, uh, come back tomorrow, for I must have time to （7.　　　　） this

（8.　　　　　）."

錫樵夫："You've had（9.　　　　　）time already."

稻草人："We won't wait（10.　　　　　）minute."

膽小獅："Not another minute!"

*第十二組測驗解答：

1. travelers　2. gate　3. empty　4. dome　5. done

6. bucket　7. think　8. over　9. plenty of　10. another

聽力測驗

冒牌貨、騙子

第十三組聽力測驗：　　　　　　　　　　CD * 13

旁白：There was a big（1.　　　　　）standing in the
（2.　　　　　）of the Throne Room. The Lion's
roar so（3.　　　　　）Toto that he knocked
over the screen. And standing in the
（4.　　　　　）the screen had（5.　　　　　）
was a little old man, with a（6.　　　　　）head

and a（7.　　　　　）face.

桃樂絲："Who are you?"

奧茲："I'm Oz, the — the Great and — and Terrible? But don't hit me — please don't hit me — I'll do anything you want me to."

桃樂絲："But I（8.　　　　　）Oz was a great big Head."

奧茲："Oh, you're wrong. You see, I've been （9.　　　　　）."

桃樂絲："Making believe? Aren't you a Great Wizard?"

奧茲："Oh, shh, shh, shh, my dear, don't speak so （10.　　　　　）, you'll be（11.　　　　　）— and I'll be（12.　　　　　）. See, I'm... I'm supposed to be a Great Wizard."

桃樂絲："Aren't you?"

奧茲："Oh, oh, not a（13.　　　　　）of it, my dear; I'm just an（14.　　　　　）man."

稻草人："You're more than that, you're a （15.　　　　　）."

奧茲："（16.　　　　　）so. Yes, uh, I...I am a humbug."

稻草人："You seem quite（17.　　　　　）yourself, you

should be（18.　　　　）what you've done."

奧茲："Oh, I am — I certainly am. I have no magical powers at all, see, so I cannot keep my promises to you."

桃樂絲："I think you're a very bad man."

奧茲："Oh no, my dear, no, no, no, I'm really a very good man, I'm just a very bad Wizard."

稻草人："Mr. Oz, you are going to keep your promise to me, I want my brains."

奧茲："You do? Hmm, well, well, uh — the（19.　　　）of you leave, if I am to（20.　　　）this magical thing, I must work（21.　　　）."

＊第十三組測驗解答：

1. screen 2. corner 3. startled 4. spot 5. hidden

6. bald 7. wrinkled 8. thought 9. making believe

10. loud 11. overheard 12. ruined 13. bit

14. ordinary 15. humbug 16. Exactly 17. proud of

18. ashamed of 19. rest 20. perform 21. in secret

頭腦、心、勇氣

第十四組聽力測驗： CD ＊ 14

旁白：When the（1.　　　　　　） were gone, the old
humbug（2.　　　　　　） the Scarecrow's head,
and filled it full of（3.　　　　　　） flakes. As he
put the head back on, he said,

奧茲："Uh,（4.　　　　　　）, you will be a great man,
for I've given you a big helping of bran-new
brains."

稻草人："I'm feeling much（5.　　　　　　） already."

旁白：Then Oz called in the Tin Woodman and gave him a
new heart of red（6.　　　　　） and（7.　　　　　）.
He gave the Lion a（8.　　　　　） of a（9.　　　　　）
that really wasn't very（10.　　　　　）, but he
（11.　　　　　） the lion drink it. The Lion did, and
went back to his friends happy as he could be.

膽小獅："Now I am full of courage."

∗ 第十四組測驗解答：

1. others 2. took off 3. bran 4. hereafter

5. brighter 6. silk 7. sawdust 8. dishful

9. greenish liquid 10. tasty 11. insisted

聽 力 測 驗

思考帽

第十五組聽力測驗： **CD ∗ 15**

旁白： When the Lion was gone, Oz said to himself,

奧茲："Well, I am glad I can make them happy, but it'll take more than（1.　　　）to get Dorothy back to Kansas. I must（2.　　　）my thinking cap. Ah, I have it!"

旁白： Next day, a very sad and（3.　　　）Dorothy was called to the Throne Room. There she found Oz（4.　　　）from（5.　　　）to ear.

奧茲："Ah, well, young lady, I think I've found the way to get（6.　　　　）out of this country."

桃樂絲："Oh, that's wonderful. Oh, thank you, Mr. Oz, but you said 'us'. Are you going too?"

奧 茲 ："Oh, oh,（7.　　　　）. You see I'm（8.　　　　）being such a humbug, and besides I want to be in the（9.　　　　）again."

桃樂絲："I see, how are we going to get away?"

奧茲："Oh, we'll make a（10.　　　　）. See, that's how I got here and that's how we're going to get away."

＊第十五組測驗解答：

1. imagination 2. put on 3. unhappy 4. grinning

5. ear 6. us 7. absolutely 8. tired of 9. circus

10. balloon

熱氣球

第十六組聽力測驗：　　　　　　　　　　CD ＊ 16

旁白：So for the next three days, Dorothy and the Wizard（1.　　　　）on a beautiful balloon. It was made out of green silk, and it was more than（2.　　　　）feet high.

奧茲："Oh, if I say so myself, it's a beauty! Now, now, now, we'll build a（3.　　　　）under it, and the（4.　　　　）will fill it up. You people there, uh, tie this, uh, rope to the（5.　　　　）so the balloon doesn't fly away."

桃樂絲："Mr. Oz, have you seen Toto, I can't go（6.　　　　）him."

奧 茲："Uh, no, I haven't, but you'd better（7.　　　　）and find him, because the balloon is filling up fast, it's beginning to（8.　　　　）on the rope here. It's ready to go. I'll get in the（9.　　　　）. The

Scarecrow, uh, uh, get Dorothy."

稻草人："Dorothy, Dorothy."

桃樂絲："Here I am, I found Toto, I'm coming."

奧茲："Oh, oh, uh, the rope — uh, I'm going up......"

桃樂絲："Wait for me, wait for me."

奧茲："I can't, I'm on my way. Good-bye!"

桃樂絲："Now I'll never get home!"

＊第十六組測驗解答：

1. sewed 2. twenty 3. fire 4. hot air 5. stake
6. without 7. hurry up 8. strain 9. basket

聽力測驗

葛琳達

第十七組聽力測驗： CD ＊ 17

旁白： But the Scarecrow had an （1.　　　　　）.

稻草人："You have the Golden Cap, why not call the Winged Monkeys? Have them take us to Glinda, the Good Witch of the South."

桃樂絲："Oh, what a good idea. Your new brains are really（2.　　　　　）. Let's see now, first my left foot, 'Ep-py, pep-py, kak-ky!', and now my right foot, 'Hi-lo, ho-lo, hel-lo!', now both feet, 'Ziz-zy, zuz-zy, zik!'."

旁白：And in no time at all, Dorothy and her friends were（3.　　　　　）to Glinda's Palace. She saw them at once.

葛琳達："My friend, the Good Witch of the North told me you might（4.　　　　　）. How may I help you?"

桃樂絲："I so want to go to Kansas, Good Witch of the South. Aunt Em and Uncle Henry must be very worried about me."

葛琳達："That's the（5.　　　　　）thing in the world. You could've gone anytime you'd wished if（6.　　　　　）you had（7.　　　　　）."

桃樂絲："Known what?"

葛琳達："The secret of the silver slippers you are（8.　　　　　）. Click the heels together three

times, and they will take you（9.　　　）you
wish to go."

桃樂絲："Really?"

葛琳達："Really. You say good-bye to your friends and
one minute（10.　　　）you will be home."

桃樂絲："Home? Home in Kansas?"

葛琳達："Home in Kansas. So say good-bye."

旁白： Then, suddenly Dorothy（11.　　　）that
she was leaving her dear friends（12.　　　）.

＊第十七組測驗解答：

1. idea 2. working 3. on their way 4. pay a visit

5. simplest 6. only 7. known 8. wearing

9. anywhere 10. later 11. realized 12. for the last time

＊左頁，葛琳達對桃樂絲說："You could've gone anytime."
CD 裡唸成 "You can've gone anytime"，不太合一般文
法。

回家

第十八組聽力測驗： CD * 18

桃樂絲："Good-bye, Scarecrow."

稻草人："Good-bye, Dorothy."

桃樂絲："Good-bye, Tin Woodman."

錫樵夫："Good-bye, Dorothy."

桃樂絲："Good-bye, Cowardly Lion."

膽小獅："Good-bye, Dorothy."

桃樂絲："I love you all."

旁白：She（1.　　　　）her friends, and then took Toto in her arms, and（2.　　　　）the （3.　　　　）of her silver shoes together three times.

桃樂絲："Take me home to Aunt Em!"

桃樂絲："Oh, where am I?"

艾姆嬸嬸："Dorothy! Dorothy!"

桃樂絲："Aunt Em."

艾姆嬸嬸："We've been looking（4.　　　　）for

you. Where in the（5.　　　　）did you come from?"

桃樂絲："I came from the Land of Oz, Aunt Em, and I'm so glad to be home again."

＊第十八組測驗解答：

1. hugged 2. clapped 3. heels 4. all over 5. world

影視歌裡的《綠野仙蹤》

　　學英語，為何要多讀經典（the classics）？因為經典歷久彌新。有些英語字眼，出自經典，英語人士說話或為文，隨手拈來，但在一般辭典裡找不到任何解釋，常令非英語人士摸不著頭腦。

　　所以說要多看書，閱讀經典名著，學英語才會進步。

　　就從我最近兩個月看的幾部英語電影及電視影集來說吧，真想不到，居然有如此多部影片，對白裡出現《綠野仙蹤》的影子。如果沒有讀過《綠野仙蹤》，可能就看不懂，或者根本不知道自己看不懂。

芒虛金

　　電視影集：《慾望城市》第三季第 2 集〈政治 vs. 性〉（Politically Erect）

　　關鍵字： Munchkin

珊曼莎在酒吧裡結識一男子，在答應對方約會時，因雙方都坐著，她沒留意到男子的身高。直到他站起身，身材高大的珊曼莎發現，男子的個子矮小，差不多在她肩膀下。

珊曼莎對眾女友說，她有點後悔答應對方：

可是，我不能因為他**個子矮**就取消約會。

But I can't cancel the date just because he's a **munchkin**.

芒虛金是誰？這個字出自《綠野仙蹤》。

當一陣龍捲風吹來，把桃樂絲從家鄉堪薩斯吹到一個陌生的國度。她的房子落地時剛好壓死了壞女巫，解救了一群受女巫奴役多年的芒虛金。

芒虛金的個子比較矮小，但還是比「侏儒」（dwarf）或「矮子」（midget）高一點。在《綠野仙蹤》裡，芒虛金好像長不高的小孩，跟十二歲的桃樂絲一般高。芒虛金老了以後，看來像小老頭和小老太婆。

成龍和他的夥伴吃了什麼？

電影：《尖峰時刻 2》（*Rush Hour 2*）

關鍵字：Toto

　　黑人警探卡特（克里斯·塔克飾）跟著他的夥伴李警探（成龍飾）來到香港，一時眼花撩亂。李警探叮嚀他要小心點，香港的幫派人物可不好惹。

　　卡特不以為然，他來自洛杉磯（L.A.），當地幫派也相當有名，他可見多了。李警探只好跟他說明白，來到香港，已非屬他的地盤，現在他只不過是個平民老百姓罷了：

> 在中國地盤，我就是麥可·傑克森，而你是**托托**。
> In China, I am Michael Jackson, and you are **Toto**.

　　據說廣東人和香港人什麼都吃：有腳的除了桌腳，所有的雞除了飛機。從卡特警探的下面這句話，猜猜看，他們昨晚去吃了什麼東西：

> 我們昨天晚餐吃了**托托**。
> We had **Toto** for dinner last night.

　　「托托」是《綠野仙蹤》裡的那隻狗，所以你大概已經知道他們昨晚吃了什麼。

桃樂絲

電影：《一曲相思情未了》（*The Fabulous Baker Boys*）

關鍵字： Dorothy

　　貝克兄弟平日以在夜店彈奏雙鋼琴為生，日子不算好也不算差，就這樣過了十幾年。

　　可是時代變了，光是彈鋼琴已滿足不了客人胃口。為了增加人氣，他們新招募一名女歌手蘇西（蜜雪兒‧菲佛飾），從此有歌聲、有音樂，三人行，果然接到更多的生意。

　　這回他們接到一家渡假飯店的邀約，地點在另一城市。出發當天，他們帶著行李，開上高速公路。蘇西閒著，隨手翻閱飯店的宣傳小冊子，興致盎然地唸著：「每一個房間都像遠足，像豪華的盛會。踏出房外，一片私人大陽台……」她忍不住驚呼出聲：

　　天啊！這地方簡直像『**奧茲國**』。

　　Jesus, this place is like **Oz**.

　　法蘭克（傑夫‧布里吉飾）瞧一眼她手上的小冊子，冷冷的表情似乎在告訴她，宣傳廣告都是騙人的。不過，既然

來了就回不了頭：

歡迎上路吧，**桃樂絲**。

Welcome to the road, **Dorothy**.

* 稻草人：前、後、左、右的模樣。

黃磚道

　　美國的報章雜誌常引用《綠野仙蹤》裡的字眼「黃磚道」（Yellow Brick Road），以下是一篇航空管制文章的摘錄，有興趣者可以上網看全文，請搜尋幾個關鍵字即可：

Commercial airline pilots know how to get from Los

Angeles International Airport to Chicago-O'Hare: They follow the **Yellow Brick Road**.

The aerial highway between L.A. and Chicago has something in common with the convoluted path in **The Wizard of Oz**. At first, the route runs relatively straight through California and Nevada. But then it slants sharply northeastward through Utah and into Wyoming to avoid traffic outbound from Denver. After a hard right turn, it winds through South Dakota, Iowa, and southern Wisconsin before descending toward always-busy O'Hare.

＊Yellow Brick Road ：此處形容此路艱險難行。

＊鮑姆家中有一箱子的戲服和假髮，兩個兒子經常作各種裝扮表演。

著名搖滾歌手艾爾頓・強（Elton John）在七〇年代發行一套專輯《再見，黃磚道》（*Goodbye Yellow Brick Road*），裡面就有這首受歡迎的歌曲：

When are you gonna come down?

When are you going to land?

I should have stayed on the farm,

I should have listened to my old man.

You know you can't hold me forever,

I didn't sign up with you.

I'm not a present for your friends to open,

This boy's too young to be singing the blues.

So goodbye yellow brick road,

Where the dogs of society howl.

You can't plant me in your penthouse,

I'm going back to my plough.

Back to the howling old owl in the woods,

Hunting the horny back toad.

Oh I've finally decided my future lies

Beyond the yellow brick road.

…………

給老師及家長的建議
——如何使用這本書

給老師

　　這本《綠野仙蹤》實際上是一齣舞台劇的對白，角色鮮明，情節活潑生動，適合學生在課堂上作對話練習，增進英語口說的能力。更可以讓學生活學活用，擇場地排練，演出一場師生共賞的戲劇。

　　聽力測驗部分，可隨時挑一章節，放 CD ，給學生作聽力測驗，作為學習英語的其中一種方法。

給家長

　　英語聽力是要靠個人時間的投入。耳朵長在小孩頭上，若光靠老師上課是絕對不夠的，所以要盡量抓住零碎的時間來聽英語。比如說，每天開車送小孩上學的途中，隨時播放有聲書，就不用擔心塞車了。長久下來，累積的聽力程度將很可觀。

　　家裡有立體音響設備，更好。把英語有聲書當成音樂或歌曲播放，隨時享受聽的愉悅。

知識性、故事性、趣味性的 英語有聲書

《英文，非學好不可》

所附的有聲書〈美女與野獸〉&〈仙履奇緣〉，Level：3

學不好英文，是許多人心中的痛。

為什麼學了多年英語卻「聽不懂，說不出，寫不來」？
問題出在哪？

本書提供現成的「教材」，一步步教你「方法」，聽、
讀、說、寫，同時進行。

至於毅力，就要靠你自己了。《英文，非學好不可》教
你做個英文贏家。

《躺著學英文 2 ── 青春‧英語‧向前行》

所附的有聲書＜搭便車客＞，Level：6

他從紐約啟程，沿著第66號公路往西行，目的地是加
州。一路上，有個男子一直向他招手，想搭便車，他到
底是誰？為何甩不掉他？不管車子開多快，他總是隨後
跟來……音效逼真，一口氣聽到最後一秒，不聽到最後
結局不甘心。

《躺著學英文 3 ── 打開英語的寬銀幕》

所附的有聲書＜搭錯線＞，Level：5

夜深人靜，一個行動不便的婦人獨自在家。她要接線生
幫她接通老公辦公室的電話，不料搭錯線，她竟偷聽到
兩個人在電話中談一件即將發生的謀殺案，就在今晚十
一點一刻整，他們打算採取行動……CD的後半部特別加
上中英有聲解說，打開讀者的耳朵，只要聽聽就會。政
大英文系主任陳超明教授專文推薦。

Studying系列15

成寒英語有聲書1——綠野仙蹤

編 著─成寒
主 編─莊瑞琳
美術編輯─周家瑤
執行企畫─曾秉常

董 事 長─趙政岷
出 版 者─時報文化出版企業股份有限公司
108019台北市和平西路三段二四○號三樓
發行專線─（○二）二三○六─六八四二
讀者服務專線─○八○○─二三一─七○五・（○二）二三○四─六八五八
讀者服務傳真─（○二）二三○四─六八五八
郵撥─一九三四四七二四時報文化出版公司
信箱─10899台北華江橋郵局第九十九信箱
時報悅讀網─http://www.readingtimes.com.tw
法律顧問─理律法律事務所 陳長文律師、李念祖律師
電子郵件信箱─popular@readingtimes.com.tw
印 刷─勁達印刷有限公司
初版一刷─二○○三年十月十三日
二版一刷─二○○九年五月二十二日
二版十九刷─二○二四年五月二十四日
定 價─新台幣三三○元
版權所有 翻印必究（缺頁或破損的書，請寄回更換）

時報文化出版公司成立於一九七五年，
並於一九九九年股票上櫃公開發行，於二○○八年脫離中時集團非屬旺中，
以「尊重智慧與創意的文化事業」為信念。

ISBN 978-957-13-3982-5
Printed in Taiwan

成寒英語有聲書. 1,綠野仙蹤/成寒編著.——
初版. ——臺北市 : 時報文化, 2003[民92]
　　　面 ； 公分

ISBN 978-957-13-3982-5（平裝 & 光碟片）

874.59　　　　　　　　　　92017005